CORPSES & CORSETS

USA TODAY BESTSELLING AUTHOR
RACHEL RAWLINGS
& MISTY SIMON

Corpses & Corsets

by

Rachel Rawlings
&
Misty Simon

Copyright page
Published in the United States
Copyright © 2024 Rachel Rawlings and Misty Simon

All rights reserved

Cover copyright © 2024 Misty Simon

No part of this publication may be reproduced, storied in, or introduced into a retrieval system, or transmitted in any form, or by any means (electronic, mechanical, photocopying, recording, or otherwise) without written permission of the copyright owner.

The scanning, uploading, and distributing of this book via the internet or any other means without the permission of the owner is illegal and punishable by law. Criminal copyright infringement, including infringement without monetary gain, is investigated by the FBIO and is punishable by up to 5 years in federal prison and a fine of $250,000.00. Please purchase only authorized editions and do not participate in or encourage piracy of copyrighted materials. Brief passages may be quoted for review purposes if credit is given to the copyright owner. Your support of the author's rights is appreciated.

This is a work of fiction. Any resemblance to person(s) living or dead is completely coincidental. All items contained within this work (names, characters, places, incidents, etc.) are products of the author's imagination.

From Rachel

For my family. Life is hard. It's harder when you're alone. Thank you for going on this adventure with me!

For my Word Witches, Misty and Laura, thank you for lending an ear, a shoulder and your creative spark whenever mine is in danger of going out.

For Laura T - the doppelganger - thank you for being a friend.

From Misty

Huge thanks to my Wordy Witches! You're awesome! Your support and belief in this from the beginning is nothing short of astounding! Lort, we finished!

This was born between us, Rachel, and I am so freaking tickled that we ran with it! May it be just the beginning of something fabulous.

To my wonderful Boot Squad for critiquing and loving, and especially Natalie for going with the crazy things I asked for to make this book absolutely beautiful!

CHAPTER 1

Guilty. A verdict at last. And not a moment too soon. Her reputation had been horrible enough before becoming a widow. Being convicted for her husband's murder would have sealed her spot on the ton's blacklist for the rest of her life. Not that Coriander cared for the opinions of the aristocratic throng who were always so eager to marry off their children for land and title. She'd taken a husband years ago at the insistence of her own parents and look where that had landed her.

Falsely accused of murder, an outcast of society, and at odds with her in-laws, despite proving her innocence and seeing the real villain brought to justice.

Coriander retrieved black gloves from the reticule fastened about her wrist and slipped on one, then the other before descending the stone steps outside the courthouse. She'd borne the brunt of society's accusatory stares and whispers, the societal papers leaving no scar untouched, all the while grieving her husband, Ezra Whitlock, and the life she had lost with his death.

She was of a mind to march straight from the Old Bailey to *The Chronicle* and demand a retraction for the way they had dragged her entire life and name through the mud. After all, their love of scandals and lack of investigative skills were as much to blame for her social decline as the man who killed her husband. A man who had been all too happy to lay the blame at Coriander's feet in the hopes of stealing her husband's archeological claim in the sands of Egypt and any treasure uncovered in the excavation. A man who had professed to be her husband's best friend and business partner, though that was proven false today in the courts when he'd been convicted of murder. And rightly so. Timothy Revelson could rot in that cell for the rest of his life for all she cared.

Actually, he was very lucky she was unwilling to risk the physical penalty for using her powers to conjure up a curse on him while he sat in a cell. She'd been very tempted to do just that and to hell with the "return to her threefold" payment...

Especially since she had once loved him as a brother, as Ezra had for years.

"I thought that was you." A familiar crisp baritone interrupted her thoughts of revenge and stopped Coriander in her tracks.

Another man who probably would have been happy to lay the blame of her husband's death at her feet, only because it would have filled his coffers. Or so he thought. She turned on the heel of her boot and directed the ire for everyone who had wronged her at her brother-in-law.

"It surprises you that I came to witness the conviction of my husband's true murderer for myself? Forgive me if I don't believe everything I read in the paper. I find their sources to be most unreliable." Her anger and accusations simmered just below the surface, ready to be released, even as she knew she could never, no matter how much she wanted to.

She wouldn't have expected anything less than this man's betrayal either. William Whitlock hadn't shed a single tear when the news came that Ezra had been killed in Egypt. He never asked if she was okay or if there was anything she might need now that her whole life had been turned upside down. He had only wanted to know when she was planning on giving him the reins for all the assets.

The answer to that had been, and still was, never, but that wouldn't stop him from eventually asking. The toff had fallen out of favor due to his unscrupulous business practices and wanted her out of the way of an inheritance he'd believed to be rightfully his.

"Come now, Coriander. We've been over this before. You can't possibly blame me for believing the worst. It was in *The Chronicle*, after all. Not one of those rubbish periodicals. *The Chronicle*." William peered over the rims of his spectacles, looking down his nose at her as he smoothed the lapel of his waistcoat.

No, she couldn't blame him for believing it. He was weak-minded. But she could, and did, blame him for spreading the vicious rumor in the first place.

"What is it you want, William?" she asked, though she knew the answer she received would not be the truth.

"Can a man not inquire as to the well-being of his brother's widow?" William's arched brows all but disappeared under the brim of a hat that matched his boring brown suit and scuffed boots.

It rankled her that men in mourning weren't required to adorn themselves in black the same way or for the same length of time as a woman was.

"He can when his curiosity is genuine." Coriander grasped her black cloak, receding into the warmth of its fur lining against the cold that held London in its bitter grip.

"Of course, it's genuine." William's tone said otherwise. He was building up to something. The same thing. As he always did. "How could it not be? What with you all alone at Elmcroft. The estate is so large and the upkeep... Well, I would hate for you to overburden yourself with its management."

And there it was.

The reason her brother-in-law had continued to hound her. She'd inherited the house upon Ezra's death. Not William.

"Elmcroft is not a burden, and I have my dear husband's memory to keep me company." Coriander loosened the strap of her reticule and fished out enough coins for a hackney before turning her back on her brother-in-law and descending the last steps to the carriages for hire parked on the street below. "Always a pleasure, William."

She felt his fiery gaze on her as she paid the driver, gave instructions to take her to Elmcroft, and climbed into the carriage without bothering to lower the step.

Coriander took her seat then sat upright with perfect posture until the carriage turned the corner. Despite the boning of her corset digging into her sides, she refused to show any weakness or discomfort. It wasn't until the courthouse and William were well out of sight that she collapsed against the threadbare seat, velvet worn away from overuse, and let out the breath she'd been holding.

Because the journey was expected to take about an hour, she let the carriage rocking back and forth lull her into a state of calm she'd rarely felt since Ezra's death.

It was done. Over.

The unburdening of a guilt that wasn't hers to bear washed over her, leaving her with a sense of weightlessness. She could almost feel the sun's rays on her face, as if the smoke that hung over the city in thick clouds had parted just for her. But spring was a long way off and even then, the sun was hard-pressed to break through.

As she'd expected, the ride to Elmcroft took the better part of an hour over muddied streets clogged with carts, pedestrians, and other carriages. Plenty of time for Coriander to worry about this upcoming visit with her cousin Florence, who went by Flossie. Even though she was only a few years older than Cory, she tended to treat Cory like an underling or a fledgling who needed her guidance and care. Of course, Cory appreciated her concern, but she also would be fine on her own and she most certainly did not need to re-enter society, which was Flossie's main objective over the next six weeks.

Taking a deep breath, she decided instead to plan her next garden plot, shifting dread to the promises of new life in the broad patch of dirt below the kitchen window at home. With a little magic and a lot of tending, her garden had become the envy of households from the Great Park to St. James Street.

But she never dared share the secrets of her botanical success. Spirits may have been welcomed into the industrial age, but witches had not.

The shunning she experienced when her peers believed her a murderess was nothing compared to what she would have experienced if they knew she wielded true magic. After they'd been married for some years, Cory had shared some of her secrets with Ezra, but never anyone else outside the family. Her family, not his.

But Ezra had never asked many questions about what she could do or how she could do it. He'd been enthralled with his machines and his digs, and that had been fine with her. She'd never used it in front of him, and it was a secret she intended to take to her grave—or the gallows. Whichever came first.

The clip-clop of horse hooves slowed, the carriage rocking forward as the driver stopped at the gates of Elmcroft Manor where Esther, her maid and closest confidant, waited in the drive to greet her.

Esther Jones was the last remaining servant at Elmcroft. It seemed Coriander had inherited her along with the house because she stayed long after she'd been told her workload would likely increase while her wages remained the same. The silver-haired woman, with a strong back and gentle smile, had taken the news in stride.

Elmcroft was Esther's home as much as it was Coriander's.

William had been correct. The gray stone manor house and its grounds were extensive, along with its upkeep. Ezra had left her little debt but also few funds, only enough to barely take care of the house and grounds. Coriander kept tight reins on her purse and a frugal budget—preferring to take up the slack in the scullery and kitchen over the expense of a large staff. They'd also shut off most of the house that they no longer used, keeping two bedrooms, the sitting room, and the kitchen open for the most part.

"Good morning, miss." Esther kept up appearances while within earshot of the hackney driver, falling back into their casual manner of conversation once he'd disappeared back down the lane. "Well, don't keep an old lady waiting. Out with it. Are they going to hang the bastard or not?"

"Esther! If I didn't know better, I'd think it was your husband Mr. Timothy Revelson had murdered and not mine." Coriander's mouth parted in a tender smile as she looped her arm through Esther's, resting her hand in the crook of her elbow as they strolled toward the house.

"If only I'd been as fortunate in marriage." Esther returned the smile, lines deepening in the corners of her eyes. She'd served this house and cared for Ezra in her own way. His death had taken a toll on her as well. "Now, are you going to tell me what happened or make me wait to read about it in *The Times*? I won't buy *The Chronicle* to fund their nasty business."

Esther hadn't purchased an edition of *The Chronicle* since the first headline bearing the Whitlock name had been printed. Cory doubted that would change unless they printed a very eloquent apology and begged for forgiveness. And she doubted even more that would ever happen.

"Guilty." Coriander gave the elderly woman's elbow a squeeze before untangling their arms to open the heavy oak door. "Shall we celebrate with tea?"

As soon as she touched the brass handle, the thing swung open. On its own...

"I thought we fixed this," Cory said, stepping inside and placing her reticule on a chair so she could approach the mechanical arm attached to the door.

Esther blew out a hefty sigh. "I keep pulling it apart and it keeps getting put back together. I don't know who or what is doing it, but the darn thing never stays disassembled."

Cory sighed, but quieter. Ezra had been many things: a good provider, an excellent husband who let her do as she pleased when she pleased, a passable cook if he was feeling adventurous. He was also an inventor of strange things, usually involving nuts and bolts, and they rarely if ever worked the way they were supposed to. Ever since his death, more of these inventions had seemed to show up on a weekly basis and no matter what she tried to do, she could not get rid of them or turn them off. She'd have to try harder.

Clapping her hands together, Cory turned from the mechanical arm. "Tea for guilty! I'm so glad that's over and now we can figure out what to do going forward. I'm just happy the wretched man is behind bars."

"About bloody time. Pity they put an end to public hangings. I'd have gone down to the square to watch him swing." Esther shut the door behind her and hurried to take Coriander's cloak and gloves.

"Esther." Coriander pretended to scold her and barely contained her laughter as she breezed through the front parlor and into the service hallway that led to the kitchen. And nearly tripped over a floor sweeper that was merrily sucking up dust from the carpet under their feet, trailing a piece of a carpet she was pretty sure resided in the next room. She wasn't even going to look. She could deal with it later. "Is there cake left?"

"A couple of slices." Esther cut her off at the pass and slipped into the kitchen ahead of her. "I'll put the water on. You fetch the teacups."

"It's a lovely day. Let's take tea in the garden." Coriander retrieved two cups with matching saucers from her best set of china from the cupboard and set them on the tray with two wedges of lemon cake. A knife came flying through the air and embedded itself into the drawer at her hip. A soft whir began behind her, part of a machine Ezra had designed to help chop vegetables that instead used anything in here as target practice. Without turning around, she snapped her fingers and the noise stopped, the machine shutting down, not because she'd turned it off but because she'd magicked it off.

A small headache began forming about her left eye with the use of her magic, but she'd take it this time.

Esther finished preparing the tea and filled their favorite pot that was hand-painted with an intricate floral pattern and set it on the tray between the cups and cake.

They ignored the ominous roll of thunder and oppressive clouds, refusing to allow the threat of another storm to ruin an otherwise beautiful day, as they bundled up in coats and took their tea outside. Cory led the way on the path between all her lovelies she'd planted and tended and gave care to, including watering and a little extra sun if she had to. The hemlock was thriving, along with the strychnine and the nightshade. As much as her garden was the envy of the ton for its beauty, it was also feared as the deadliest, and no one actually knew what was in here, except her. She kept it that way intentionally.

Arriving at the small, white wrought-iron table with its two chairs in the center of the garden, Cory set down the tray and breathed in the fragrant air. Now that the trial was over and the verdict finalized, she could refocus on getting her life back together. Not in the way Flossie wanted her to, but in a way that suited her. She'd looked forward to many better days because there hadn't been enough of them since Ezra died, and Coriander doubted there would be many more with her cousin due to arrive for an extended stay later that day. She'd take what peace she could get when she could get it.

Flossie had insisted on staying with her until she had her feet under her and a man back on her arm.

Coriander was happy to have her for the former but had absolutely no interest in the latter. They'd sort that out later.

Except, Coriander heard several sets of horse hooves clopping up the drive and Flossie's voice a bullhorn as she shouted out orders before the conveyances even stopped. She was yelling for maids and servants, kitchen help and livery men to take up the call and get her unpacked so she could rest and get a look at the amount of work that would need to be done before she could be comfortable.

Cory closed her eyes as she forked up the last bite of cake. The fact that she could hear her cousin all the way in the back of the house, not to mention all the way in the middle of her deadly garden, did not bode well for the coming days. Perhaps she'd just come up with a way to distract her once she saw her. First, she wanted to get into the house before Flossie set her army free and knocked over or tripped over any number of contraptions Ezra had made but the world was not yet ready to see.

"Honestly, Coriander, it's immoral. Not to mention forbidden." Flossie righted the framed photos throughout the parlor that had been turned face down after Coriander's husband died. "It's no wonder there was suspicion and talk of curses."

Her cousin gestured to the whole of her, head to toe. Cory had found a way to distract Flossie, but she was afraid she might have miscalculated and started something she was not ready to handle.

"When, exactly, did you become an expert on morality?" Coriander tugged the corner of the black veil, watching as it slid down the front of the mirror to pool at her feet before revealing her own reflection. In for a penny, in for a pound. "Besides, what could possibly be said about me now that hasn't been said already?"

"Oh, I don't know... That you're a witch?" Flossie scooped up the black fabric and bundled it to her chest.

"Are you going to tell them?" Coriander arched a quizzical brow and peered back at her cousin through the mirror. "Your maiden name is Thornback too if I recall."

"My husband wasn't murdered under suspicious circumstances." Flossie sighed and squeezed the fabric tighter to her bosom. "How am I supposed to introduce you back into society if you refuse to play your role accordingly?"

"I don't know, but it won't be in black widow's reeds. I'm too pale for mourning clothes." Coriander half turned in front of the mirror, examining the fit of the bold black-and-burgundy-patterned dress from all angles. "The robbers could avoid the grave and snatch me straight from my bed."

"Perhaps the lavender dress then?" Flossie pointed to one of the dresses that had been cast aside on the chaise lounge.

But Cory didn't want subtle or demure. She wanted liberation and to be able to move on now like everyone else seemed to have done.

"Ezra left for Egypt two years before he died." Coriander missed her husband, the ease with which their lives intertwined without stifling the other, and the security their marriage provided, but she'd said her goodbyes a long time ago.

And on the nights she longed to see his face and hear tales of his adventures in the land of the Pharaohs, as a witch, she was not without the means to do so.

If she was willing to pay the price.

"Well?" Flossie demanded with a huff, tossing the black cloth she'd been clutching onto the bed beside a pile of rejected dresses. "What are you intending to wear to her funeral then?"

Another funeral. Flossie had handed the missive over when she'd alighted from the carriage two hours ago. It had been slipped onto the bench up top of the carriage when they'd been stopped in the middle of town. Flossie hadn't wanted to hand it over, but she hadn't been able to stop Henry, her coachman, from doing so. And now she wouldn't be able to stop Cory from paying her respects to Franny Michaelson, a childhood friend she'd lost contact with until recently.

London was ripe with the dead or dying and as cruel and it was, Coriander had grown tired of grieving, but she would not miss sending off her friend into the afterlife even if she hadn't seen her in years.

But this death was different from the others. Even that of her husband. The dearly departed was a witch and though she wasn't a Thornback, Coriander felt obligated to pay her respects.

It was the least she could do for an old friend. Especially given their past.

CHAPTER 2

Flossie chattered away at Cory the entire way to the funeral at the small cemetery on the outskirts of town. She spoke of balls she would be working on getting invites to, teas that should be set up, soirees she'd like to host at the manor, and visiting the modiste to secure appropriate dresses for each occasion.

Cory looked out the window of the coach Flossie had insisted they use. According to her cousin, the ton simply did not rent hackneys to take them places. Any other day, Cory would have scoffed at Flossie and her rules and restrictions in regards to the ton. When Ezra had been alive, Cory had been blessed to stay out of the upper realm of society, content to tend her gardens and keep the estate running on her own. She'd not been invited to any teas or balls after her first year of flat-out refusing every single invitation without explanation. They'd gotten the hint for the next year and her silver server at the front door had remained—thankfully—empty.

But what Flossie was suggesting would mean Cory would have to make small talk with people she had no interest in, conform to a society's rules she had no time for, and smile when she had nothing to smile about.

"And then we'll make sure to get in touch with Sir Edgington, he's recently without a wife and would make a fine match. He has two children who need raising so you wouldn't have to worry about securing a line." Flossie tapped Cory's knee with a fan that perfectly matched her brown and cream day dress. She was not coming to the funeral with Cory, but would just be there to make sure she came home after.

The carriage bounced along the road to town. The sound of the horses' hooves striking the road gave Cory a headache, but she wouldn't miss saying a final goodbye to a woman she'd run in the fields with as a child.

"Absolutely not on Edgington. His wife's spirit visits me regularly, so regularly in fact that I had to ask her to make it only weekly. I found I couldn't get a single thing done with her wailing. It was akin to a banshee. I'm almost certain he had her killed, since I'd caught him skulking around my herb garden."

"You didn't!" Flossie smacked her knee with the fan.

"I did." Cory turned from the window and removed Flossie's fan from her dress, smoothing out the burgundy and black fabric. She'd chosen something that would celebrate the woman being put to rest while also being respectful of the occasion. She'd also tucked a sprig of pressed freesia into her sleeve to slip into the grave before the first shovel of dirt was placed on her coffin. It would help with the journey to the next plane and also signal that she'd never forgotten her. Cory just hoped she wouldn't also visit her, so she'd put together a spell on the flower to keep the spirit from being restless.

And she'd make sure it was sealed and activated just as soon as they got to the cemetery.

"Are we taking the long way?" Cory asked, realizing they'd gone past the same building for the third time. She knew she should have told Flossie she'd take the hackney.

"Of course not." But Flossie wouldn't look her in the eye, and after what seemed like only a minute later, they arrived right at the cemetery that was but one block past the building.

Knowing that avoiding things was not going to make them go away, and that Flossie was often completely incapable of minding her own business, Cory took her hands and rested them on her knees.

"I truly do understand what you want to do. I also get the role you want me to play, and that being seen at a funeral for a prostitute is not going to get me those invites you so desperately want for me. But I have to do this, cousin. Too many people in my life have been dying. None of them are connected, but if I don't acknowledge and mourn each then I'll be stuck in a cycle I can't break."

"There are other ways to break the cycle," Flossie responded, squeezing Cory's fingers.

"I can't and I won't do that." She straightened in her seat and reached for the handle of the door. But the thing was opened from the outside by a footman, another thing Flossie had refused to send away when she'd arrived at Cory's.

At first, Cory had only thought they were there to drop her cousin off, even with all the yelling. She'd thought they'd get a room ready for Flossie and then make their way back to the home her cousin shared with her husband. But then Esther had been in a frenzy trying to find bedding for the servants' quarters upstairs that hadn't been used in years, even before Ezra had left on that last, fateful trip. The many spiders who'd decided to make the back stairs their home had been swept clean of the forgotten hallway.

Esther still was not happy that Flossie had brought an entire staff with her. And Cory wasn't going to make them pay for their mistress's lack of foresight. She had no idea how she was going to feed everyone, but Flossie had immediately put her maids to work cleaning and dusting every room, pulling the sheets off the furniture in rooms that hadn't been used in two years.

Cory had stopped her when they got to Ezra's study and demanded the room not be touched, then pocketed the key to the door and walked away.

And now it was time to walk away again. This time from Flossie. But now she was walking toward yet another grave. She hadn't been certain where exactly the burial was to be held, but she wasn't overly surprised that it was on the very edge of the cemetery, right up against the stone wall.

There were five other people there besides the pastor who was overseeing the burial. Cory recognized the three women from when she'd visited Franny Michaelson one afternoon in an effort to get her to come work in her gardens and give her another path to consider. But Franny hadn't wanted to give up her chance at some sort of windfall she'd been promised.

And yet two weeks later here they were after she had fallen down a staircase supposedly. Esther had finally told her that she'd heard of the death but had not wanted to tell Cory due to the circumstances and the life Franny had chosen.

Cory planned on talking with the ladies after the service was over about exactly whose staircase that was.

She arrived in the middle of the pastor reading the lord's prayer and fought back the urge to flinch. Franny had not only been a prostitute, she'd also been someone who had first taken her oaths seriously to harm none but found a way recently to skirt those restrictions and toe the line of acceptable.

Had that been what had her taking the stairs faster than she'd meant to when someone pushed her?

Cory shook off those questions and glanced up at the sky, willing it not to rain before she had a chance to get her flower in the coffin.

"Today, we meet here to wish safe passage to Francesca Michaelson. Her life was not always easy, but I was told she did the best she could with what she had." The pastor took a cloth out of his breast pocket and wiped his brow. Was he afraid the devil himself would bring the fires of hell up here to roast him for telling such blasphemous stories on a sacred ground?

Cory almost laughed. There were worse things.

But she kept her own counsel and waited until he was done talking to approach the casket. She also waited for the other three women to move away before she slipped the flower out of her sleeve and placed it in the crack under the lid of the coffin. That way even if this was a drop-bottom coffin, one that was used over and over again to show a modicum of respect to the deceased if they couldn't afford a casket of their own, the flower would not be lost.

To the right a contraption began whirring and spitting out steam. It clanked and clunked as it lowered the coffin into the ground. It reminded her of something Ezra had created early in their marriage and made her smile, just a little.

That smile dropped when she realized the small group of women stood apart from Cory in their own circle. She'd hoped to speak with them about Franny's death, but she didn't want to intrude on their grief.

Her gaze wandered around the desolate setting, taking in the drooping trees on this side of the plot of land, the way the grave markers listed left or right as if not solidly in the ground. She wished she could have done something to make the grave better but had only found out at the last moment that her friend had died. That missive that Flossie had not wanted to hand over had been a news clipping of a prostitute's death and handwritten note with the time and location of the funeral.

She'd asked questions of Esther, who had reluctantly told her that it was true Franny was gone and that she'd hoped Cory wouldn't find out.

And now her childhood friend would only ever be a memory from this moment forward. Well, hopefully, with the help of that freesia she'd only be a memory and not a spirit that haunted her. Cory had taken to locking down the house with spells and incantations along with salt at every window since Ezra's death. But with all these new people in the house she might have to explain herself, so she'd have to step up the incantations and rely more on the magic than the everyday remedies.

The whirring turned to a churning sound and then a loud thud. The machine seemed to seize and the rope pulled tight, snapping at the last second as the bottom of the coffin dropped and Franny rolled out into the hard-packed dirt under her.

One of the women screamed and another fainted. The pastor mopped his brow again, and Cory was close enough to hear him muttering to himself.

She stepped closer.

"I was not paid enough to deal with this atrocity. She should have gone on the other side of the wall. This is what happens when you desecrate God's holy ground with women like..." He trailed off when he caught sight of Cory's narrowed eyes. His gaze darted away and he raised his hand in the air.

As if by magic—and Cory knew magic—a man appeared with a chest of tools. His eyes darted left and right as he hit the machine with a hammer and then clanked it with the side of his hand. He couldn't seem to keep his gaze off the woman's body in the grave.

Cory looked into the hole and her eyes watered as she saw the cheap and chintzy dress they'd buried one of her oldest friends in. It looked like something from the back of a madame's closet that might have been in season twenty years ago. Her hair was a mess and they'd done nothing to fix the side of her head where it had been caved in. From the stairs? A banister?

An attack?

Cory stopped herself from thinking too much about that. There was nothing she could do for her friend now except mourn what could have been.

But having buried her husband, she knew what could be done to make a corpse look peaceful, at rest, almost as if they had just fallen asleep. And none of that had been done for Franny.

She didn't want to break the circle of women who probably didn't remember her and had every right to snub her when they themselves were mourning the death of a recent friend. But she had to ask.

"I'm so sorry for your loss," she said, standing back from them in case they did not want her to join them.

The redhead darted a glance over her shoulder but then smiled and turned fully, her figure pulled tight in a dark-brown dress that had seen better days. "Now, you're Coriander then, aren't you? Seen pictures of you when you were much younger. Just went through them for Franny here the other day so not everything got throwed away."

Franny still had pictures of them? That hit harder than seeing her tumbled into a grave, for some reason.

"Yes, we grew up together."

The man at the machine stopped working, seemingly intent on listening. For what, Cory had no idea, but he gave her the chills and she always trusted those chills.

"Can I interest you all in a cup of tea and a small gathering to talk about Franny? I'd like to know more about her now and perhaps what happened to her, if you know."

The one with the dirty, brown hair and a black dress that shone in the sun in spots where the velvet had worn off laughed bawdily. "You'll need something stronger than tea if you want that story."

CHAPTER 3

"Honestly, Flossie." Coriander reached over, snatched the fan from her cousin's hand and turned to apologize to the women packed together on the opposite bench in the coach. "She's always had a flair for the ridiculous."

"Me?" Flossie's eyebrows disappeared beneath the rim of her bonnet and a tear leaked out of the corners of her eyes.

Not from offense at Coriander's words but the smell of the women perched on the seat across from them, probably.

Flossie pinched her nose and turned toward the window, muttering about which of them was the ridiculous one, and did her best to ignore Coriander and the guests in her coach.

There was no denying the pungent aroma of body odor beneath the watered-down French perfume and alcohol that permeated the cabin of the coach, but the information Coriander required was far more important than her cousin's delicate sensibilities.

Coriander had offered a few coins to the footman in exchange for the flask stowed in his coat pocket.

Flossie had argued with Coriander over whether her driver would have liquor on his person at all, but Coriander knew from casual conversations with the hackney drivers she'd hired over the previous months that it was cold on the streets of London and the whiskey kept the chill in their bones at bay.

Flossie had not been amused by this discovery and threatened to replace the driver should he continue to drink under her employ. Coriander reassured the man his position was secure and pressed another coin into his palm.

A little something to loosen their tongues and increase the flow of conversation. Coriander took a small sip from the flask and held back the cough that worked its way up from her chest as the harsh liquor burned its way down.

She caught her cousin eyeing the small silver container filled with cheap whiskey as she handed it to one of the prostitutes seated across from her and pursed her lips to hide a smile.

"So, you're wanting to know how Franny ended up in that coffin, I reckon?" The redhead took a long pull from the flask before passing it to her friends.

"Obviously." Flossie's eyes narrowed to slits as she pried her fan from Coriander's iron grip. "The sooner you satisfy her morbid curiosity the sooner we can return home to a proper tea in a respectable parlor."

"Hear that, girls? She doesn't find our company respectable." The redhead snickered and reached for the whiskey. "Ain't that just like a toff. Bet her husband would disagree."

"How dare you speak of my husband in such a—"

Coriander leaned forward, interjecting herself into the argument brewing between two hot-tempered women in close quarters. Things were not unfolding as she'd hoped. Coriander needed to regain control of the conversation or risk returning to Elmcroft with nothing more than a headache and a sour stomach to show for her efforts.

"I'm sorry, I know we met briefly during my last visit with Franny, but she failed to introduce us properly. You know my name, but I regret I do not know yours." Coriander continued to address the redhead who seemed to be the one in charge, or at least the one the others deferred to when speaking with a relative stranger.

"Katherine Murray, but you can call me Kitty. Everyone else does." She extended a hand covered in a fingerless lace glove, frayed at the edges and a size too small. The stained ivory crochet barely grazed her knuckles.

"I bet they do. *Oomph*." Flossie pressed her palm against her side where Coriander's elbow had found its mark.

"It's lovely to make your acquaintance, Kitty." Coriander clasped her hand around the other woman's and held it for a moment. "What can you tell me about Franny's death? I must admit, seeing her spill out of the coffin like that was rather upsetting."

"Rattled your nerves a bit, did it? You're not the only one. Poor priest looked like he'd seen the devil 'imself." After she cackled at her own words, Katherine upended the near empty flask over her open mouth until the last drop plopped onto her tongue. "Serves him right. Judge not. Lest ye be judged. That's what the good book says, innit?"

"Something like that, yes." Coriander held her own beliefs and spent little time around an open Bible, but that was a sentimentality she could agree with. "About Franny," she prompted, hoping to encourage the conversation forward before the tiresome events and company caught up with her. Coriander much preferred Esther's company and the quiet of an empty home—something she knew she wouldn't enjoy for several weeks.

"Franny took a tumble down the steps. That's what the constable says. Pushed, is what I say." Kitty crossed her arms over her chest as her friends nodded in agreement.

The coach rocked back and forth as the driver circled the block once more. Coriander was running out of time and her cousin out of patience.

"You think she was murdered?" Coriander's chest tightened as if someone were cinching the laces on her corset. She fell against the back of the seat and sucked in a breath, gathering her wits about her now that her previous thoughts had been confirmed. "Murder. But why? She had no money. No real prospects. At least not for the long term."

"Well, she had one, dinnit she?" Kitty sucked air between her jagged teeth. "Never trust a man, 'specially one like 'im."

"Like him? Him who?" Coriander demanded, unable to contain her curiosity. Was this the windfall Franny had spoken about? "Did you see him? What did he look like?"

Not for the first time, Coriander wondered what type of man Franny had become involved with and what sort of promises he made to make her comfortable enough to lower her guard. The residents in the Westminster rookery aptly named Devil's Acre were not a trusting lot. Franny was no exception.

"Why you so interested in Franny all of a sudden? She some kind of a charity case to you or somefing?" Kitty jiggled the empty flask. "Don't s'pose there's any more refreshments?"

Flossie scoffed and shook her head. Her cheeks were flushed and she appeared ready to launch into a tirade and eject the women from her coach. Coriander couldn't help but wonder if she'd be tossed out along with them.

"More's the pity," Kitty said when no one produced another drink. "Never saw him meself, at least not his face. He kept his collar up and his cap down. Knew how to stick to the shadows. But he had more than a few coins in his pocket. Left Franny flush whenever he visited."

"Wish I could find a mark with full pockets like that." The blonde woman squished against the carriage door grumbled under her breath.

"Then we'd be burying two of you, wouldn't we?" Rolling her eyes, Kitty tucked the flask beneath the folds of her skirt, daring Coriander to argue for its return with the indelicate move.

"So, this mysterious man paid Franny a handsome sum of money each time he visited her? And you're certain he visited more than once?"

"I've got eyes, don't I?" The woman raised her chin and tilted her head to one side. "He was clever enough to hide his face but carried the same cane. Had one of them fancy glass knobs on the top, and he wore a shiny silver ring with some sort of crest."

"A crest?" Coriander glanced at her cousin, hoping to see the same excitement over this latest development that she felt but Flossie's attention lay elsewhere.

She seemed more concerned with people milling about. No doubt concerned that someone would recognize her carriage. The frequent trips around the block would feed the gossips for at least two days.

Coriander almost felt pity for her cousin, but a scandal over her carriage circling the block was a far cry from what she'd experienced before clearing her name. If Coriander could survive that, her cousin surely would survive a few rumors that she seemed to be a little too interested in one block in town.

"Can you describe the crest?" Coriander asked, hoping to glean some unique detail that would lead to the identity of Franny's mystery man.

A man who may well be the prime suspect in her murder, or at the very least, the last person to see her alive.

Coriander reflected on that a moment and based on the manner of Franny's death decided that he would almost have to be one and the same. But why?

"Sort of looked like an eye." Another shrug and then Kitty smoothed out her ragged skirt. "That's all I could make out."

"An eye?" Flossie scoffed, turning her head from the window long enough to rejoin the conversation. "That seems a small detail for you to have noticed while crossing someone's path."

Flossie dismissed Katherine's observational skill with a wave of her hand and returned her attention to the bustling streets packed with cart mongers and hurried shoppers. While her indelicate nature left much to be desired, she raised an interesting point.

How had Katherine noticed such an intricate design if not in close quarters with the man himself?

"It was an unusual piece. It was the emerald that caught my eye. The design of the eye was almost like something ancient-looking, like they put on those flyers for the museums around here. The walking stick had a big knob on top." Katherine narrowed her gaze on Flossie as if in challenge.

Flossie accepted. "Now that I can believe."

"Bloody toff." The brunette who'd been otherwise silent throughout the carriage ride spat at Flossie's feet and rapped her knuckles against the roof. "Thanks for the drink, Miss Coriander. I think it's best we be on our way."

The driver eased the horses to a stop beside a cart laden with fruits and vegetables. As the three women disembarked from the carriage, they descended upon the merchant. Katherine and the blonde sweet-talked the fruit monger while the brunette helped herself to the apples, hiding them within the layers of her skirts in a masterful maneuver of misdirection—one they'd no doubt practiced on numerous occasions. They disappeared into the alleyway with the fruitmonger none the wiser.

"She knows something, something else about Franny's man that she's not telling us." Coriander turned her attention from the empty alley and focused on her cousin. "You were terribly rude to our guests. Katherine might have offered more information had you made even the slightest attempt at cordiality."

"Our guests?" Flossie's cheeks flushed a shade of red that rivaled the apples piled high on the fruit cart. "You are welcome to invite whomever you'd like into your home, but last I checked this was my carriage and I don't recall agreeing to escorting those women around the streets of London."

"I think all of the balls and champagne bubbles have gone to your head, Flossie."

Coriander reached across the seat and took her cousin's hand in hers with the hopes of settling her nerves and softening her next words. It wouldn't do to have her cousin upset for long. Coriander feared the consequences, which would no doubt involve hosting a tea or worse yet, a ball at Elmcroft.

"You and I were one marriage away from a life of destitution, Flossie. We mustn't forget that. If anyone discovered who we are or what we can do, our fates would be far worse than theirs. There but for the blessings of the Goddess go I."

"Yes, well... It would have been nice of you to at least ask for the use of my carriage." Flossie settled the matter and acknowledged the truth in her cousin's words with a squeeze of her hand and a soft smile.

"I should have asked where they were staying. You don't suppose they'll take over Franny's room, do you?" Coriander chastised herself for the oversight.

It was all too easy to disappear in London's rookeries. Finding Franny's friends would prove difficult if she needed to speak with them in the future.

And she had more than a feeling that she would. Her intuition was rarely wrong.

"Coriander, tell me you're not planning to invite them to tea. I understand your point, I do. And while I agree to an extent, you know as well as I do that you would not survive another scandal. And if you want to keep that scoundrel of a brother-in-law at bay, and keep ownership of Elmcroft, you will need to secure yourself a husband."

"Don't worry, cousin. I have no intention of causing a scandal." Coriander meant every word. While she had no designs for a new husband, she agreed with Flossie's opinion on the status of her reputation.

Her independence and magical abilities relied upon her ability to remain out of the papers—and the courtroom.

Still, Franny's death left her unsettled. Making a few additional inquiries into the manner in which her old friend met her end seemed the least Coriander could do.

Her mind was made up. Coriander would visit Franny's room, track down Katherine, along with the two other women, and find out what else they remembered about the mystery man. She was certain Franny's friends had more information to share.

After all, Katherine had already provided enough details to eliminate the constables' usual suspects. Residents of the rookery where Franny lived weren't likely to own an ornate walking stick or wear an emerald ring—at least not for very long.

The ring was of significance. Coriander knew it as well as she knew that her friend hadn't fallen down those stairs.

It wasn't a name or a face, but it was more than Coriander could have hoped for—somene else who thought that Franny's death wasn't an accident. Her intuition was not out of kilter.

She shouldn't have doubted herself, and had it not been for the several months she'd spent under the scrutiny of the public eye and the constabulary, she wouldn't have.

Still, she had clues, a description of sorts, and she knew just who to take them to. He owed her a favor, and it was time she collected it.

CHAPTER 4

Evading Flossie upon their return to Elmcroft proved much harder than Coriander expected. From the moment the coach pulled to a stop alongside the stone steps, she'd tried and failed to make excuses for her absence so that she might slip out of the house. It was a long walk to the constabulary. The sooner she started her journey the better.

Her cousin, however, would hear none of it.

An hour later, under Flossie's watchful eye, Coriander was still sitting in the parlor sipping a cup of her personal blend of feverfew and ginger root tea for the migraine she'd pretended to have and now felt brewing for real.

"I think I'll go lie down for a bit." Coriander placed her teacup on the small table next to the couch and rose, smoothing the folds of her dress in an effort to dodge Flossie's accusatory gaze.

Coriander had honed her ability to keep secrets—a skill paramount to the survival of any witch—but she'd never mastered the ability to deceive those who knew her best. Especially when they shared the same magical abilities.

"You are aware, of course, that I know of every escape route in this house and that includes the trellis descending from your bedroom window to the gardens below? I played here as a child, too, dear cousin, we were all in the same circles. I can actually see it from here if I twitch the curtain just a fraction. It's why you never won at hide-and-seek." To prove her point, she moved to said window and flicked the fabric back just enough for Coriander to see that her preferred landing spot was right in their line of vision.

"Yes, well, I was the reigning champion of Sardines." She'd won the reverse hide and seek game and Ezra's heart in the process.

He'd been the first to discover Coriander's hiding place in the small pantry beside the scullery during the first and last game of Sardines she'd ever played. She'd caught him admiring her over tea and, having found him handsome enough, returned his smile with one of her own. She was relieved when he'd been the first to find her and surprised to find how much she enjoyed his company while they waited for the other players to locate them. The fifteen minutes she'd spent alone with him in the cramped cupboard had been the most exhilarating of her young life. Ezra engaged her as his equal right from the beginning. They'd been friends, and that had meant more than anything to her as they'd moved through life together. She would have been fine with that status quo for the rest of her life except that he was taken so abruptly.

Coriander sighed, both in frustration from the loss of her husband that continued to loom over her and from her domineering cousin. Flossie ignored her, and refused to give an inch, counting off the rest of Coriander's exit routes on her fingers.

"I also know about the back door from under the kitchen, the side door leading out to the stable, and the window that opens out onto the garden. Oh, and the escape panel that leads into the secret passage you asked Ezra to put into the walls, as well as the window in your conservatory that can be removed and used as an exit."

"Flossie, you are a pain in the ass."

Her cousin had the audacity to laugh. "I think a donkey might be offended by that statement even if I'm not. Now, sit down and finish your tea. Esther went to a lot of trouble to make sure it was the right temperature and had the right amount of sugar in it. You shouldn't disrespect her by leaving it to cool for too long just because you'd rather be out helping someone who not only did *not* ask for your help but is also dead so couldn't ask anyway."

"That's boorish." Coriander stuck a hand on her hip.

"And yet not untrue."

She couldn't dispute that, but she was a grown woman, for goddess's sake and did not have to give an account of her every movement. She hadn't even had to do that when she was married to Ezra. They'd lived happy lives both together and apart, and he trusted that she would do the right thing at the right time. Although if she were honest, she was almost positive he would be just as against her going after clues to find a murderer as her cousin was.

"Sit." Flossie gestured at the couch. Coriander chose to take her teacup and sit in a chair farther away.

"Stop being a petulant child. Those women are more than welcome to try to sell you any story they want, and if you pay for their alcohol, give them free rides in my coach as opposed to having them leave as they had arrived, on foot, then of course they'll try to rope you into any number of things. I may not approve of their profession, but you cannot dismiss the fact that they must be some of the best actresses in today's world given how they have to pretend to like sleeping with some truly horrible men. I'm barely able to fake it effectively with my dear John and he still hasn't figured out what exactly he's supposed to be doing. I can't imagine having to coo and grunt with some penny-pinching, handsy oaf on top of me." She flicked open a fan and began flapping it rapidly.

"Speaking of the deed is making you overheat?" Coriander said slyly while looking at her from the corner of her eye. She hid her small smile behind her teacup when Flossie scoffed.

"You are not going to distract me from the conversation we're having. You cannot go out and get involved in something that does not involve you and could possibly be a hoax. You have no true information that would point to a murder, and you are not equipped to find one. Plus, you need to be concentrating on re-entering society. Ezra may have provided many things during your lives together, but he left you with far more than you can handle and not enough funds to even have a staff to properly care for it."

Coriander sputtered in protest.

"Not a full staff." She arched that eyebrow. "Beyond that, his brother is harassing you, and you would do better to keep your eye on the things that are important to you and your survival, not looking for someone who might want to kill you also to make sure you don't talk if you get too close." She harrumphed and snapped the fan closed. "I'm just trying to protect you, you ninny."

Coriander let that sit for a moment because Flossie had always tried to protect her, and out of all her family and even extended family, she had always been there. But she didn't understand this time. Perhaps if she explained herself...

"I do appreciate everything you've done and do, my dear cousin. And I know you have my best interest at heart, but something is telling me that this is more than it appears to be, and I don't think I can let it go." She took a deep breath that pushed her skin against the chafing corset. "I don't want to put myself in danger, of course, but I have someone who owes me a favor, he's reputable, and he would be the perfect person to ask questions in quarters where a lady such as myself would not be welcome, much less tolerated. I'm not an ignoramus. I know what my limits are, but this is something that's calling to me, and I feel I can only ignore it at my own detriment."

Another scoff, but this one also had a hint of intrigue exhibited by Flossie's raised eyebrow. "Is this *someone* part of the ton? Though he can't be if he's accepted in the circles you are looking into."

"He's well-connected and aboveboard. Why must you always doubt me?"

The other eyebrow went up.

"Fine, I will admit that I have sometimes been impetuous and done things that on second thought were probably not my best idea, but there's something here, Flossie. I have to at least ask around to see if anyone knows what happened."

That wasn't entirely true, but little white lies seemed to be her forte more than big falsehoods. While connected and respected, Inspector Wiley Parker's calling tray had no doubt remained empty. Still, he was Coriander's best chance at uncovering the truth about Franny, and the man was indebted to her after the humiliation he'd caused during poor Ezra's death investigation.

Flossie shook her head and snapped the folded fan against the arm of her sitting chair. "I'm not going to be able to stop you no matter what I do. You'll just get more inventive in your schemes."

Coriander waited her out because there was no good answer to that one without showing her hand.

"Do what you must, but please be careful. And for goddess's sake, take my coach. No more of this renting hackneys when we have two perfectly acceptable conveyances right at this house." Flossie rose from her chair and smoothed her skirts. "I'll leave you with something to consider before your little adventure. I'm not going anywhere until you re-enter society. Be warned that the more time you spend on this matter, the longer I'm here."

She all but floated over the floor as she steam-trained her way out into the hallway calling for Jessica, her personal maid, to ready a sleeping aid that Coriander was almost positive was nothing more than a shot of aged brandy, so she could relax in her room.

Coriander wasted no time hauling herself out to the kitchen to have a quick talk with Esther, who also wanted her to be careful, and then talk with the footman whose spirits she'd acquired earlier to see if he'd be willing to take her to the office of one Special Inspector Wiley Parker.

Not long after, they were on their way to the constabulary. She had no real plan other than to ask him to make inquiries around the death of Franny and find out anything he could about the cane and the emerald ring. Being a botanist meant that she had often drawn flowers and other vegetation she came upon in the forest when she was out exploring. She'd done her best to capture the image of both items to be able to show him. She wished she could stop by to show the drawings to Katherine first to confirm that they were what she'd seen, but she knew better than to visit one of the rookeries so late in the afternoon.

She sat in the coach, smoothing the edges of her drawings over and over again, as she waited for the driver to get them through the late afternoon traffic and to the constabulary before the inspector left for the day. Heavy rains the night before left the roads rutted and rough, which made her grateful that Flossie had not insisted she had to attend with Cory. She preferred being tossed around the inside of the carriage without incessant complaints from her cousin.

When they pulled up at the door of the constabulary Coriander asked Henry, the valet and driver to wait for her around the corner. In her mind the inspector was indebted to her for the slight against her reputation and she intended to press that upon him. Her cousin's grand coach would do little to convince him of her plight.

The Metropolitan Police headquarters' massive brick and stone building jutted up from the street. The tips of its turrets and dormer windows pierced the London fog and the clouds above. Windows wrapped the building but if her memory served, Parker's office was on the second floor of the east wing. She saw no activity up there from her limited vantage point on the street but knew from experience activity bustled inside the walls. Her shoulders back and spine straight, in part due to the overtightened laces of her corset, Coriander drew in a breath of fortitude and made her way up the stone steps.

She removed her hat and her gloves upon entering the vestibule, then took the flight of stairs up to the second level. She marched through the halls with the confidence of someone who belonged, which she most assuredly did not. Coriander wasn't a constable, criminal, or even an average citizen. She was a practicing witch and risked discovery by bringing herself to Inspector Parker's attention once more.

But she'd convinced herself that Franny was worth it, and with her mind made up, there was no turning back.

The death of her friend wasn't just another of London's senseless murders. It meant something. Of that much Coriander was sure, and she intended to find out what that meaning was.

Finally, she arrived at the inspector's door and drew in a deep breath before rapping her bare knuckles on the solid wood. It wasn't that Special Inspector Parker was disagreeable that set her nerves on edge. When he wasn't insistent upon her guilt in Ezra's death, she found him reasonable enough. It was more that she preferred not to draw attention to herself, and when she felt compelled to do so it was usually for a reason she'd rather not be pursuing.

But Inspector Parker owed her, and she was there to collect as much as possible. Whether he liked it or not.

CHAPTER 5

"Unless you're the superintendent himself, it would be in your best interest to quit knocking on my bloody door." Special Inspector Parker shouted his warning from the other side of the solid oak slab. And then he yanked open the door with enough force to create a small draft, swishing the hem of Coriander's skirt over the threshold of his office. "My apologies, I mistook you for one of my constables. How may I be of assistance, miss?"

His question trailed off on a groan when he looked up and found it wasn't a random Miss, but a Mrs. that stood outside his door. One he was all too familiar with and probably didn't want to see ever again. He'd expressed his gratitude to be done with Coriander when the true identity of Ezra's killer had been revealed. As far as Cory was concerned, the feeling had been mutual. She'd have been fine to never see him again.

Until someone else she cared for had been murdered. Coriander's business with the inspector wasn't finished. Not by a long shot.

"Do you address all your callers this way, Inspector?" Her grip on the sketches tightened, threatening to crush the delicate paper in her hand. "It's a wonder any crime is reported at all with greetings like that."

"Ms. Whitlock, to what do I owe the pleasure?" The inspector ground out the last word between clenched teeth and a forced smile. He stood in the doorway, blocking her entrance to his office.

Whatever Coriander planned to say, she would have to say it while standing out in the hall. She cleared her throat and raised her chin, meeting the steely-eyed gaze of the special inspector with one of her own.

"I recently attended the funeral of a dear childhood friend," Coriander began her explanation. "We'd lost touch over the years until recently, but after speaking with her acquaintances I feel her death was unnatural and warrants further investigation."

"Do you know what I find unnatural, Ms. Whitlock? That the people you care about seem to meet an untimely demise that warrants further investigation." He hooked his thumbs around the straps of his suspenders and hoisted them over his shoulders before fastening the top button of his shirt.

Coriander recoiled at the harshness of his words. "Well, then you should count yourself lucky to not be among them."

Her visit to the inspector's office was not going as planned.

"Forgive me, Ms. Whitlock." He let out a long, slow breath and raised his hands in a placating gesture. "It was a busy night and a busier day, even by London's standards."

"That's no excuse for your utter lack of manners. However, as I once again find myself in need of your assistance, I will overlook this latest slight." Coriander fought the urge to smile.

She'd been offended at first, but his poor manners provided the perfect opportunity to appeal to his male ego by asking for his help while ensuring she received that help with the guilt over his past transgressions.

"How very kind of you." The inspector's furrowed brow and deep-set lines around his mouth led Coriander to believe he didn't think her kind at all.

She feared she'd made the trip across town in error, wasting her time and proving Flossie right in the process. And that would not do. She would demand Inspector Parker's attention, and for however long she had it, she would make the most of it.

"Of course, Inspector. Think no more of it. The matter is already behind us." Coriander returned her attention to Franny's gruesome demise. "As I was saying, a childhood friend met her end, and I believe foul play was involved."

She would withhold specific information, such as Franny's name and the name of the rookery where she rented a room, until she had a commitment from the inspector to investigate. Coriander had little good to say about the inspector, but he was a man of his word. If he agreed to look into the manner of Franny's death, he would.

As long as she got him to agree before he knew the victim was a prostitute who had supposedly fallen down the stairs.

Coriander knew all too well about the deep-seated prejudices held by many of the God-fearing constables. She'd experienced it firsthand after Ezra died. Franny was a woman, a witch, a prostitute, and poor. That was one strike too many against her character.

"What of this friend, then? You believe she was murdered?" Inspector Parker reached inside his door and plucked his jacket from a rack to the left of the doorway.

"Yes, I believe she was. Franny found herself living in a less-than-desirable neighborhood. She—"

"Excuse me, did you say Franny?" The stitching on Inspector Parker's coat sleeves strained against the wool fabric as he shoved his arms in with more force than necessary. "Please tell me this is not about the harlot who died in the rookery? You think she was murdered? Because that case is closed as an accident, Ms. Whitlock."

"Just because she fell on hard times doesn't mean the circumstances of her death do not warrant an investigation." Coriander poked the inspector in the chest with her drawings. "She was involved with a man and—"

"More than one, no doubt. And the only thing your friend fell on was her back." Inspector Parker ignored Coriander's gasp, grabbed the end of the rolled-up drawing papers, and ripped them from Coriander's hand. "People die in the rookeries every day, Ms. Whitlock, and the circumstances are rarely a mystery."

"But there are witnesses. If you'd allow me to show you my sketches of the description they provided." Coriander pointed to the paper still clutched in the inspector's hand.

"Witnesses? No one spoke to my men. Why haven't they come forward then?" He tugged at one end of the bow, removed the ribbon, and unfurled the papers.

"I can't imagine why," Coriander muttered under her breath.

She struggled to tamp down her temper and the magic that built within her. If Coriander were a lesser witch, she would have hexed the inspector and been on her way, but she wanted justice for her friend. Using her powers in such a manner would not serve her cause.

Still, the longer she stood in the inspector's doorway listening to his vitriol the greater the risk of tapping into her magic and revealing her own secrets became.

Her cousin would be beside herself if Coriander lost control. She'd never hear the end of it. The mere thought of being subjected to one of Flossie's lectures was more than enough for Coriander to keep her magic in check.

"What are these?" Inspector Parker held out a sketch in each hand. "A crest and... Is this supposed to be a cane? I thought you said you had a description?"

"Those are the descriptions. That crest is a vital clue to the identity of the man that murdered Franny." Coriander tapped her index finger on the sketch of the ring Katherine had described to her earlier that day.

"Ms. Whitlock, I'm sure you have fond memories of the deceased from your childhood, but this isn't evidence of a murder." Inspector Parker stacked the papers, one on top of the other, rolled them back up, and handed them to Coriander. "After the manner in which you lost your husband, it's understandable that you've succumbed to your emotions. Go home, Ms. Whitlock. Mourn your friend, and your husband, and leave any investigations to the constables."

Coriander felt the heat of her anger flushing her cheeks as she met his gaze and leveled him with her best glare. "Good day to you, sir. "

She snatched her sketches from the inspector's hand, spun on her heel, and marched herself out the same way she came in with her chin out and her head up. She ignored the snickers and sideways glances as she passed the constables who'd gathered in the hall. Coriander refused to give Inspector Parker the satisfaction of humiliating her.

The days of caring for others' opinions of her had long since passed. Which meant her cousin had her work cut out for her if she intended to reintroduce Coriander to society.

The idea that rooted itself in her mind as she navigated the busy street to the coach waiting for her around the corner was proof enough of that.

Coriander had intended on returning home at the end of her meeting with Special Inspector Parker as she'd promised Flossie, but after being disregarded the way she had, she was in no mood to return to Elmcroft and the lecture that no doubt awaited her.

A new plan had formed entirely by the time she reached the carriage, and she gave the driver the address of her next destination.

"Are you sure, Ms. Whitlock?" The driver's face puckered as if he'd tasted something sour. "I don't think my mistress will appreciate my taking you or her coach into the rookery."

Was she sure? Coriander paused on the coach step and contemplated her plan to investigate Franny's murder on her own.

"You let me worry about Flossie. I'll take full responsibility for anything that happens." She peered over the top of the carriage door at the driver and plastered on her best, most reassuring smile. "Besides, I don't plan on staying long. I just need to ask Katherine a few more questions, that's all. We'll be home in time for supper. Everything will be fine."

Coriander ignored the flutter of nerves in her stomach as she settled into the bench seat and watched the cityscape shift outside the carriage window. The sun dipped below the rooftops, signaling a shift in the types of activities Londoners participated in.

Nothing good ever happened on the city streets after sundown. Especially in the rookeries.

Her driver wasted little time reaching their destination, pushing the horses to their limit as they navigated the other coaches and pedestrians.

Coriander's heart sank as the tenement where Franny had lived with Katherine and a handful of other women came into view. The building leaned hard to one side, and cracks ran along the brickwork like the ivy on Elmcroft's chimneys. The roof was in need of repair, as were two of the second-story windows. The front door hung on its hinge at an odd angle, leaving a gap at the top left corner. Any paint had long since peeled away, leaving the wood trim to the elements and rot.

The scent of stale sweat and urine permeated the air, and Coriander feared it would do the same to the wool fabric of her dress and cloak, giving away her location to Flossie when she returned home before she would have a chance to offer an explanation and smooth things over.

Coriander's shoulders rose and fell with a deep breath. There was nothing to be done for it. She was already in the rookery. She climbed out of the carriage, spared a few coins for the children that had gathered as soon as they'd approached, and made her way through the rickety wooden gate.

The stones that once lined the path up to the front door were evident beneath the layers of moss and mud that had overtaken the small courtyard between the street and the tenement's door. Coriander gripped her skirts, hitching them up over the tops of her boots, and made her way up the front step.

She stood outside the door, hand poised to knock, when a gentleman burst out from the other side and crashed into her, knocking her down in his haste to leave.

"I'm quite all right. No need to trouble yourself on my account, sir," Coriander shouted at the stranger who hadn't been bothered enough about her well-being to spare a backwards glance over his shoulder.

Picking herself up, she brushed the dirt and grime from her clothes and marched up the front steps. In his haste to leave, the man had left the door ajar. Coriander didn't wait for an invitation from one of the residents or bother knocking and slipped inside.

The interior of the tenement was as grim as the exterior. Cracked plaster walls and worn wide-planked floorboards met her in the foyer. She tiptoed around the pails collecting drips from the leaky ceiling and followed the wear pattern to avoid the cracks on the wooden stairs.

"Katherine?" She knocked, the door creaking open under the rap of her knuckles and announced herself. "It's Coriander Whitlock. May I speak with you?"

The tenement house was quiet. Too quiet for that time of day. The landlord was nowhere to be seen. Neither were any of the other occupants who likely lived in the other rooms on the second floor. Katherine and the others should have been finishing their preparations for the long night of work ahead of them.

Something was wrong. Coriander felt it in her bones and reached out with her magic, sensing the area around her. The energy that reacted with her magic confirmed the tingles racing down her spine.

As did Katherine's dead body. She was in a pool of blood on the floor, her body mangled, and Cory's instinct was to not only run but also be sick.

"Madam, stay where you are." A male voice shattered the silence. "The constables are on their way."

Coriander spun around, her heart pounding in her chest and skirt hem sweeping through the pool of blood on the floor.

He raised his hands, palms out, and widened his stance, blocking the doorway. "I must warn you, I am quicker than I look. Should you try to run, I will give chase, and I assure you that you won't get very far."

Coriander took measure of the formidable man across from her. He was fit and trim, his wool suit stretching over a body of corded muscle. She had no doubt about his athletic prowess or ability to outrun her.

The lack of corset laces and boot heels certainly gave him an additional advantage, too.

She paused in her assessment of the quality of his clothes, the dark smoke of his eyes, and length of onyx hair tied back with leather cording to process what he said.

"I beg your pardon? Are you accusing me of...of..." For the first time in a long time Coriander had found herself at a loss for words with the accusation that hung in the air.

"Of murdering the woman whose blood you're standing in?" From the arch of his brow and firm set of his jaw, his belief in her guilt was obvious.

"You couldn't possibly think me capable of something like this." Coriander gestured to Katherine's mangled body at her feet.

"It's hard to say what you're capable of. We've only just met."

The man smiled. *Smiled*. With a wink no less. Coriander felt her ire rise along with her magic, a spark of power reaching all the way to the tips of her fingers. But she tamped them down before she landed herself in more trouble.

She'd been accused of murder. Again. That was enough for the moment.

Coriander wasn't sure what was worse, the prospect of dealing with the constables or Flossie once she heard the news of her latest misadventure.

Magic may have been out of the question, but Coriander needed to keep her wits about her and come up with a plan—before she ended up in the back of a police patrol wagon.

CHAPTER 6

Somewhere in the back of her mind, Cory's instincts were screaming to run and never come back. There was so much blood, and she did not want to have to defend herself for something she didn't do. Again.

Dammit and if this got back to Flossie or to the inspector, she might be fresh out of luck.

Calculation was not always her forte, but she forced her belated panic back and considered very logically what she could do in the moment to escape. She could deal with the horror and sadness later, after she was far from here and this tragedy. Perhaps if she was nice to the gentleman in front of her, he'd back down from his accusations and not tell the constables that he thought she did it.

But that smile was still there, and he hadn't budged. She was pretty certain he wasn't planning on moving at all until the constable came in. Damn and double damn, even triple damn in this particular set of circumstances.

How on earth was she going to explain this to Flossie? Ha, she might be in jail and not able to tell her a damned thing. Cory went to bite her nails but realized she still had her gloves on. She stuck her hand behind her back then brought it back out. Her gloves were pristine, not a drop of blood on them.

"I've done nothing, and I'll thank you for keeping your suspicions to yourself. I have no problem waiting for the police to get here, but I will not have you slandering my name by bandying around your accusations. I don't have any blood on my person except on the hem of my dress. I would have far more if I had been the one who had done this."

He had the sheer audacity to shrug, and Cory had never had the urge to punch someone more than she did at that very moment.

Not even all the people who had thought her the one who'd murdered her husband, not even when she'd had to face Ezra's brother on the courthouse steps and listen to his ridiculous claims that he should own part of the money Ezra had left behind.

But this man, this unnamed stranger who was keeping her from escaping a place she shouldn't have been in the first place, if she had one lick of sense, was seconds away from getting that smirk permanently removed from his chiseled face.

Maybe she had finally hit her threshold of stupidity and he was going to be the one she took all her frustrations out on.

Fortunately, or unfortunately from the frown on his face, Inspector Parker showed up at that moment. The long look he gave her and the way he sighed did nothing for her fear or her irritation.

He might owe her for his past behavior during her husband's murder investigation, but she had a feeling this was not going to be the time to call in the payment.

"Miss Whitlock, why am I not surprised to see you here?" He stuck a hand on his narrow hips and pointed at the floor where the blood felt like it was soaking into her shoes. "Right in the middle of a mess, again, are we?"

She scoffed because she had no words. There was nothing she could say to right this situation, and denying everything was not going to work no matter how persuasive her argument. He'd barely believed her last time until it was almost too late.

She looked around for the man with the color of raven's wings in his hair but didn't see him standing opposite her as he had been before. Had he moved? Been taken for questioning? Because she had stumbled upon the scene, but he had to have already been here to be able to point the finger at her as soon as she stepped into the hallway and then still have time to call the police on her.

"There was a man up here with me. Tall, built, dark eyes and dark hair pulled back in a que. Where did he go?"

"I don't think that's going to work twice, madam." Parker took a step closer, and she could already feel the manacles on her wrists even though he hadn't even pulled them out.

How had her life turned into this? She'd done so few things outside the realm of good. Had taken every road that had been laid out for her without questioning it out loud, even if inside she had been clamoring for something other than marrying and setting up a house instead of a garden. She'd wanted desperately to be a spinster, walking through her garden, and tending the fruits of her labor, but that would have been unacceptable, and so she'd chosen Ezra when he'd asked, even if it was not the path she had wanted.

And this was her payment? Do one thing outside of the lines of acceptability and suddenly she was a suspect in a murder of a woman she'd met with less than four hours ago?

She wanted to sigh, one of those big gusty ones that would nearly blow down a house. Instead, she merely stood there trying to figure out how she could avoid telling Flossie that she'd taken her coach and her footman, stepped in blood, gotten arrested, and wouldn't be home for breakfast. And not because she was out having a grand old time now that she wasn't in mourning.

Damn.

Parker was taking her measure as she processed what to do next. "If you'll follow me, I don't have to put the cuffs on you unless you feel you won't be able to control yourself on the way to the station." He spoke so softly she had to lean in. "This can be just a questioning from an eyewitness," he continued. "That may change after we talk but for the moment, I'm ready to listen if you're going to be honest with me and behave."

"I've done nothing wrong," she stated.

"Care to tell me what you're doing here then?"

She shook her head.

"Nevermind. We're not discussing this until I get you out of that pool of blood and into the station. Please follow me."

"I'll get blood on the stairs."

"We'll clean it up. Just follow me."

She didn't want to go but didn't see another choice.

And then there was a clattering on the wooden stairs, like a team of horses pulling a coach over cobblestones with no master at the reins.

"Do not move, Coriander."

It was Flossie, and she was brimming with rage and something else Cory couldn't quite put her finger on.

"We are in the middle of an investigation, my lady." Parker stood between her and her cousin. She wanted to warn him but didn't know what to say.

Cory caught sight of the footman she'd stolen earlier lurking in the stairwell behind Flossie. He must have gone back to the house at some point and let her know that Cory was in trouble. She was both relieved and infuriated. Relieved that she was not here alone but infuriated that he'd leave her so quickly after she'd asked him to stay put.

He gave a slight wave, and she dipped her head a fraction of an inch to acknowledge it.

As soon as Flossie smacked aside the officer blocking her from the top of the stairs, Cory knew trouble was brewing. When she felt a tingle in the air, she flinched at the amount of magic Flossie was holding in her hand. It could be epic and dangerous, and in front of the police was the wrong place to show her powers.

"Flossie."

But her cousin shook her head and released the magic into the stairwell and through the hallway in front of her. It should have felt like an enormous explosion and instead felt like a gentle breeze wafting through an open window on a bright spring day.

"Inspector Parker, is it? I remember you and the way you helped our dear Coriander once you understood the real truth of what happened to her husband. We of course don't want her to go back to a cell where she doesn't belong, as this too is an odd circumstance of fate. Coriander was with me all this afternoon and only took the carriage out for a quick jaunt around town to clear her head for the séance we're going to tonight. She meant no harm. Perhaps she heard this poor woman at our feet scream as someone killed her and came to investigate if there was trouble. I've warned her before about involving herself in things that have nothing to do with her."

At that Flossie cut her eyes Cory's way. Cory flinched again but stood firm. She wouldn't talk now, but she and Flossie were going to have a good old-fashioned brawl when she was finally released from custody.

"And you are?" Parker asked.

"As I said, I'm dear Coriander's cousin. I'm here to reintroduce her to society. She's been through so much over the last few years." A pulse of energy slithered out again. "I understand some of the early issues had to do with you and your inability to find the real culprit. But that's all behind us now and she's moved on even if I told her I wasn't sure how she could forgive so easily. But you know Coriander. Always giving everyone the benefit of the doubt."

Parker's eye twitched, and Flossie released a short and powerful dose of the magic right at him. No creeping this time.

"Ah yes, of course. I would never believe Coriander would do anything like this. It must have simply been an unhappy coincidence that she ended up here right as the woman died in a pool of blood."

Cory shot a glance over at Parker to see if he was being his normal sarcastic self but instead found him writing something down in a little notebook and then tapping it on his chin. "I do wonder about the man who was here. You said he pointed a finger at you, Ms. Whitlock. How did he get here before you to be able to do that without being a part of the murder himself?"

"An excellent question and one you should take back to the station and explore without her. I'll take her home and we'll be available if you need us, though I don't think you will, to be honest. You'll solve this without any involvement from Coriander, I'm sure about it. In fact, I insist."

Another pulse of magic, this one more of a burst instead of a push. Parker staggered backward, and Cory reached out to save him from falling down the stairs.

"That's enough, Flossie," she whispered.

"It's just the beginning, and you're lucky I got here in time. We'll talk later because I have many things to say to you. Many. Things."

Flossie turned with a flounce of her hem on the floor and yanked on Cory's arm. Cory yanked back.

"I can't walk down the stairs in these shoes. Help me take them off."

"We don't have time," Flossie whispered back harshly.

"We'd better make time." Cory was not going anywhere trailing the poor dead woman's blood through the hallway, down the stairs, onto the street and then into the carriage.

"Fine," Flossie snapped, but it didn't look fine. She waved a hand through the air, marking from north to east to south to west with her fingers firmly aligned. "Henry."

He came quickly and got on all fours in the dingy hallway. Cory had no idea why until Flossie pushed her back and she landed with a grunt on his back as if he were some kind of settee. "This is highly inappropriate!" she said.

"So is stepping in a pool of fresh blood with nothing but your slippers on. Don't talk back to me right now. I have had it up to my eyebrows with your outrageous behavior. Ezra would be appalled at the total disregard you seem to have for anything resembling a normal life for the station he left you with."

That made Cory clamp her lips together and stifle a sob as Flossie bent down to slip her shoes off, scoffing the whole time.

"We'll have to clean these. I have a few solutions in my bag that I should be able to use. You're going to have to walk down the stairs and into the street barefooted, but your hem should cover the faux paus. Just don't get any splinters, for the love of all that's holy, or I'll make Henry carry you down on his back like a child."

She stomped down the stairs as Cory rose from her seat on Henry's back. He righted himself quickly and yanked on his surcoat to look as he had when he'd first brought her here.

He took a step toward the stairs, and Cory couldn't help but reach out a hand to his forearm. "I'm so sorry for putting you in this mess," she said.

"I'm sorry I had to go tell Miss Florence. I debated not going because I didn't want you to be mad at me but in the end, I just couldn't wait when I saw the cops winging in like they'd found the gates of hell."

"Don't apologize. I'd be in a jail cell right now if it hadn't been for your quick thinking."

"Get down here. NOW!" Flossie yelled and they both hopped to. Cory was going to have a long ride back to the manor no matter how far the actual distance was. She was ready for it. Maybe.

The carriage ride had indeed been long. Flossie used the entire time to berate her over and over again and ratchet herself up both in anger and volume until Cory saw Esther standing on the front steps before they even turned in the drive.

She was wringing her hands and stamping from foot to foot. Wonderful.

"Flossie, now that everyone within ten miles knows what an imbecile I am, could we please go inside so I can wash my feet and change my dress?" She had blood crusting on the hem, but the darker color kept it from being too noticeable to the naked eye. That didn't mean she hadn't been very much aware of it with every single turn of the carriage wheels.

"You may change and wash, I'll make sure the water is ready but change into whatever you're going to wear to the seance tonight."

Cory opened her mouth and Flossie threw up a hand, the one she'd used to daze Parker back at the flophouse. "Do not under any circumstances tell me you are not going or that you're not feeling well. Or anything really, other than you'll be ready in an hour. I accepted this invitation to be able to cover up for your issues this afternoon. Do not fight me on this. I don't care if you're throwing up at this point. Bring a bag with you and make sure you don't get it on anyone. I'll see you in sixty minutes. We're heading to the Havershalls and we will not be late."

Cory marched up the stairs in her bare feet, fuming to herself. She stepped over a contraption that closely resembled a mouse but was built to pick up any buttons or strings on the floor. It usually ate wood instead because Ezra had done something wrong in the calculations, but no matter how many times she'd tried to get rid of it or lock it up, it would reappear.

And just the thought of Ezra and what she was going through now got her dander right back up to top notch.

This was her house and her stairs and her feet. Her time. She did not need to do what Flossie said just because it was Flossie saying it. She'd better get that straight with her cousin or she'd never gain her independence back.

"I do not need a keeper. And if I want to look into the murder of a friend of mine then I will look into that murder. I do not need her permission to do anything." By the time she was done complaining, she'd stomped into the room and threw her dress over her head. She stood in her shift and breathed as best she could through her tantrum.

She would go to this seance and she would do what Flossie asked her to do, but tonight was it. And tomorrow after breakfast she and Flossie would sit in the salon at the back of the house and Cory would lay out the terms of Flossie continuing to stay on. Because she was here at Cory's pleasure, dammit, and as a widow she didn't have to do a damn thing she didn't want to!

CHAPTER 7

"I'm not sure what is worse, the charlatans masquerading as true spiritualists performing seances all over town, or the hypocrisy of the people who attend them." Cory squinted out the window of the carriage as it rolled toward the Havershalls' home.

Of course, she knew the answer. The charlatans were worse.

Despite the fact that the members of the ton would as soon hang a real witch in Trafalgar Square as associate with one, no one deserved to be fleeced of their savings in such a manner. Preying on the grief of others was a horrible offense in her mind and one she hoped to put an end to. After she put an end to the murders taking place in the rookeries, of course. It seemed her calendar was filling up. Though not in the way her dear cousin intended.

"Will you at least make an effort to appear happy?" Flossie whacked Coriander on the knee with her fan before reaching into her reticule to retrieve a small glass vial. "Or shall I spike your drink with a few drops of my daisy draft?"

"Why, have you perfected it? Or would you prefer me giddy as a schoolgirl while attending the Havershalls' seance?" Coriander snatched the vial from her cousin's hand and tugged the stopper from the neck of the tiny bottle. "Perhaps I should just drink some now. It wouldn't do for any of the eligible bachelors to see me frowning, now, would it?"

"Don't be so dramatic, Cory." Flossie arched her brow and flicked her gaze from the bottle in Coriander's hand to her reticule, open and waiting to hold the potent potion once again. "Of course I don't want you acting the fool tonight, but you won't attract a husband with a case of the morbs either. It won't hurt for you to smile once and awhile."

"You accepted an invitation to a seance, Flossie. Not tea or a ball. I would think speaking with the dead is a rather somber affair. Assuming they manage to accomplish such a feat." Coriander knew all too well the cost of speaking with the dead. Which was why she went to such lengths to avoid it.

Leave it to Flossie to select this card over all the others piled up on the calling tray. It had been empty for years, but with Flossie in town making waves to those in the ton suddenly it had started filling up. Apparently, everyone else knew that Flossie was arriving but she'd neglected to let Cory know ahead of time. Disappointing but Cory should have expected it.

The carriage came to a stop outside a double-fronted brick townhouse that was home to the Havershalls.

"The courtyard is quite lovely, if not a little small." Flossie admired the black-and-white-]tiled walkway that led to a set of marble steps and the front door. "Perhaps there's more space in the garden."

"Are we here to attend a séance or add to your husband's list of properties?" Coriander teased her cousin as they ascended the stairs and rang the bell.

"We're here to find you a husband. The Havershalls' eldest son was recently widowered and is expected to attend this evening." Flossie tapped her fan against her palm as they waited for a member of the staff to open the door.

"I see." Pressing her lips into a thin line, Cory clasped her hands in front of her.

"And what is that supposed to mean?" Flossie turned her head, tilting it to one side, and narrowed her gaze.

"Honestly, Flossie." Coriander kept her eyes focused on the door, willing it to open. The sooner the night began, the sooner it ended. "Just how recent is *recently*? The poor man is probably here with the hope of speaking to his dead wife."

"Yes, well." Flossie's fan went still in her hand. "There's bound to be other eligible gentlemen here in need of introduction to a beautiful lady."

But none whose family her dear cousin had vetted.

Flossie didn't profess as much, though it was there for all to see in the frown that settled on her face. Coriander dipped her chin and hid her smile. It was a small victory over her domineering cousin, but a victory nonetheless.

The Havershalls' butler opened the door and escorted them into a drawing room where the rest of the guests were seated around an oval table.

Flossie broke off from their escort, tugging Coriander by the hand behind her to greet their hosts.

Mr. Havershall, a robust, silver-haired, eighty-year-old with a bulbous nose and rounded waist threatening the buttons of his waistcoat, was seated between his young wife of two years and a son very much in mourning. Mrs. Havershall's gloved fingers danced along the ruby-encrusted necklace adorning her throat as she welcomed the cousins to their home. The younger Mr. Havershall pulled a handkerchief from his pocket, dabbed his swollen eyes, and wiped his nose before stuffing the ivory cloth back into his pocket.

"There's no need to gloat, Coriander." Flossie muttered the words under her breath, conceding to the obvious state of grief of the Havershall heir as they took their seats.

"There may not be the need, but there is certainly the desire." Coriander tucked her skirt beneath her, slipped into her assigned seat, and waited for the rest of the guests to arrive.

And for the show to begin.

As far as Coriander was concerned, that was exactly what the séance would be. A performance to rival anything presented at The Globe.

Flossie occupied her time sipping brandy and conversing with the Havershalls and other lower-ranking members of the ton as the last of the seats were filled—save two.

Madam Olivia, a popular spiritualist of the day, made her appearance moments later with all of the theatrics Coriander expected. Draped in lavish velvet robes, the fair-skinned, dark-haired medium took her place at the table beside the younger Mr. Havershall. Her eyes were painted with black makeup similar to the paintings of the Egyptian pharaohs that decorated Ezra's study. Coriander had to admit, despite being a charlatan, Madam Olivia was quite beautiful. Which no doubt made her schemes that much easier to commit.

There was one vacant chair at the table to the left of Coriander, and she couldn't help but wonder who had rejected the Havershalls' invitation. As the gas lamps dimmed and the candles flickered to life on the table, she found herself envying the absent party.

"Everyone join hands." Madam Olivia's Romanian accent was thick, harsh, and overdone. "Tonight, I will cross through the veil and bring back the spirit of Elisbeth Havershall."

Flossie turned to her cousin with pursed lips and pinched eyes. Coriander was quite familiar with that expression and decided for once to adhere to the warning of not uttering a single word about Flossie's error in placing the young Mr. Havershall at the top of her list of potential husbands for Coriander.

She could only hope her dear cousin learned her lesson about matchmaking.

Everyone joined hands, forcing Coriander to stretch across the space between her and the guest on the opposite side of the vacant chair. The gentleman's gaze dipped below Coriander's chin long enough for him to appreciate the cut of her dress and the awkward angle she was positioned that enhanced the view of certain features. The old man was at least quick to avert his eyes once he felt the weight of Coriander's glare. She was not sure why the young Mr. Havershall stood off to the side instead of taking the chair next her, but she didn't have time to ask.

"Let us begin." Madam Olivia placed a book, a delicate handkerchief with Chantilly lace around the edge and a gold locket on the table in front of her before reciting her spiritual prayer. "Now that we have raised the spectral energy within this room, let us raise the spirit of Elsbeth—"

The click of boot heels across the marble floor broke the silence and Madam Olivia's concentration.

"Please accept my apologies for the intrusion, Madam. I hope I haven't missed anything." The late arrival removed his hat and black double-breasted overcoat and set them both on the back of the settee.

Coriander gripped her cousin's hand hard enough to crush bone, slipped her hand free of the old man on her left, and went ramrod straight in her chair.

"Cory, what has gotten into you?" Flossie hissed under her breath as she pried her cousin's fingers from around her own.

"That's him. That's the man I saw in Franny's room." Coriander kept her voice soft and low, but she felt the weight of the man's gaze as it fell upon her at the mention of her departed friend's name.

"Who? Him?" Flossie leaned closer to her cousin, whispering in her ear. "He's actually quite handsome. Not at all like you described."

"Yes, well, the devil has been known to wear many disguises," Coriander replied through gritted teeth.

"Ms. Whitlock." One corner of his mouth upturned in a mischievous smile as he arched a chiseled brow and nodded in her direction. "How lovely to see you again."

"Oh Ms. Whitlock, you've had the pleasure of meeting Larkin? I mean, Mr. Reardon." Mrs. Havershall blushed when he focused his attention on her. "How wonderful."

"Yes, wonderful. And yet, again, you are interrupting the work I do. I will ask the next host to perhaps not tell you of my visitations if you cannot show up on time and follow the rules. Again." Madam Olivia lacked the mystique and enthusiasm displayed moments ago. "If you'll take your seat, Mr. Reardon, we will begin. *Again*."

The intolerable man was light of foot and mood as he crossed the room, seemingly unaware of the spiritualist's hawkish glare trailing him as he filled the last seat at the table. It seemed Coriander wasn't the only one who did not find an introduction to Mr. Reardon to be a pleasurable experience.

Still, her curiosity was piqued by the circumstances of his relationship with Madam Olivia. While her introduction to Mr. Reardon had been brief, he hadn't struck her as someone to believe in spiritualism.

Madam Olivia regained control of the evening and her audience, instructing them to once again form a circle of energy by joining hands.

"Ms. Whitlock?" Mr. Reardon's gaze dipped to Coriander's lap, where her hands were clenched together. His palm remained open, expectant, as everyone around the table waited for them to complete the circle. "Would it shock you to know that I accepted this invitation upon discovering you would be in attendance?"

"Why, is there another murder you would like to accuse me of?" Coriander let her ire slip before good manners and judgment could prevail. "This may come as a shock to you, Mr. Reardon, but your reasons for attending this affair are as irrelevant as your opinion of me."

"Cory," Flossie scolded, before apologizing to their hosts for her cousin's emotional outburst.

Heat flushed Cory's cheeks as she became the center of attention at the party for all the wrong reasons. Even at the height of the fruitless investigation against her for Ezra's death, Coriander kept a tight rein on her temper, but there was something about Mr. Reardon that stoked the coals and ignited a fire within her.

"Of course, you're right, cousin." Coriander addressed the Havershalls and Madam Olivia. "Please accept my apologies for the interruption."

Coriander took her cousin's hand in her right and hovered her left a hair's breadth above Mr. Reardon's. To everyone else seated around the table it would appear as though they completed the circle—and appearances were all that mattered. Magic, not physical contact, was all that was required to speak with the dead.

And Madam Olivia had little if any of that. But Reardon grabbed her hand and wouldn't let go no matter how much she tugged. Not wanting to create a scene again, she stopped fighting and instead seethed as Madam spoke her words of falsehood.

The remainder of the séance went as expected, flickering candles, rattling table legs, and manifested voices from beyond the pale. Young Mr. Havershall's grief was on full display as he sobbed into a handkerchief while Madam Olivia spoke in generalities that could have applied to any widower.

Still, Coriander recognized his pain. It spoke to her heart and reawakened the aching loss she had thought was behind her. A fresh wave of sorrow washed over her and, in its wake, she made a decision entirely out of character.

Coriander tapped her magic.

Nothing overt as to out herself as a witch in society, but enough to offer some solace to young Mr. Havershall. She weaved what she knew of the deceased into the generalities presented by the spiritualist to flesh out the spirit that had supposedly been raised.

Madam Olivia's voice softened, her tone higher in pitch as she spoke truths she couldn't have known. Coriander hated giving an ounce of credence to the fraud draped in velvet and crystals, but it was a small price to pay for the peace she saw in Havershall's eyes.

The real price for using her magic had yet to be paid.

Flossie bumped Coriander's knee under the table and gave her hand a hard squeeze. She knew full well what had transpired, and there would no doubt be a conversation about it on the carriage ride home.

Her cousin wasn't the only one who seemed displeased with the séance's turn of events. Frown lines settled at the corners of Mr. Reardon's eyes and mouth. His brows furrowed together until they all but formed a single line across his forehead as he studied the spiritualist with an intense and disbelieving gaze. But when he turned those knowing eyes to focus on her, Coriander realized she may have made a fatal mistake.

She'd thought him obtuse upon first meeting him. And who could blame her? The man misread every single clue that lay before him at the crime scene. But Mr. Reardon was more observant than Coriander gave him credit for. She'd drawn the attention of a peculiar and potentially dangerous man.

With the séance concluded, Coriander was quick to decline a second glass of sherry and made excuses for her and her cousin's early departure. For once Flossie held her tongue and her questions until they were well out of earshot of the remaining party inside the Havershall residence.

"What in Goddess's name was that all about? Using magic in the home of a well-respected and well-connected family." Flossie tossed her fan and reticule onto the bench seat, climbed inside the coach, and settled in for the ride back to Elmcroft. "I hope the risk was worth the reward."

"If it eased poor Mr. Havershall's pain even a little, then the answer is yes. It was worth it. What good is having magic if we can't use it to mend a broken heart?" Coriander had asked that same question every day over the course of her own mourning period, but deep down she knew that time was the only remedy.

Still, the use of her gift was as much a comfort for her as it was for Mr. Havershall.

Coriander ended the evening with her magic and her reputation intact, but for how long? The look in Mr. Reardon's eyes worried her. There was something about *that man* that worried her. She hadn't seen the last of him, and if he suspected witchcraft, the real cost of her magic might be more than she could afford.

CHAPTER 8

As soon as they arrived back at the house, Cory shot out of the carriage after barely waiting for the door to open. If she could get up the stairs and away from Flossie, then she might be able to avoid the rebuking altogether or at least until the next day.

It almost didn't work when Flossie grabbed her elbow as she sailed into the foyer and headed for the stairs.

"Don't you dare walk away from me," Flossie said with more steel in her voice than Cory was used to. Yes, Flossie could be domineering and even took the reins right out of most people's hands, but usually that was done with a certain finesse so the person wasn't even aware they no longer had control.

But Cory knew, and while this would only give her a reprieve of a few hours, she was still willing to take it and pay for it tomorrow.

She yanked her arm out of Flossie's grasp and shot up the stairs, careful to lift her skirts so she didn't trip and fall. She had to get to her room. Now.

The feeling of grief and loss that gnawed at her stomach was the first thing to take her breath away as she slammed her bedroom door behind her. The curtains had not yet been drawn on her windows, but as night was falling and she had not lit any candles, things should be fine for what came next. Or at least the atmosphere would be fine even if she knew she herself would not be.

The second hit was a cool breeze on her neck that lifted the tendrils curling right above the line of her dress. She groped her way to the chair in front of her vanity and waited. Phase one and two of this process could be difficult but they were nothing compared to the next stage of dealing with a restless spirit.

The wailing hit her ears hard enough to feel as if her eardrums shattered. Fortunately, Cory knew that despite how loud it was, no one else could hear it. Just her. Vibrations ran up and down her spine with each moan, a discordant and almost feral-sounding groan of grief and unhappiness with the circumstances the ghost found herself in.

"I wanted to talk with him!" The shout was enough to shake the looking glass before her. Cory waited it out knowing there would be more and to move would only make it worse.

She did make sure to keep her eyes focused on her own reflection so as not to make visual contact with the woman hovering over her shoulder, keening like a banshee.

"You could have let me talk to him! I would have been able to tell him to be careful because I was not in an accident, it was murder!"

That last word had Cory flicking her eyes up to the ghost, and the connection that was made took her breath away again.

It was as if someone was shoving her soul aside inside her own body and there was no room for both of them. Cory's bones ached, and no matter how much she tried to keep her jaw clamped shut she lost control within seconds.

"I needed to make that connection," she whispered. But it wasn't really her whispering, it was the ghost of the young Mrs. Havershall. Any moment now she might be able to understand what it would take to make Cory actually speak at a normal volume, and Cory had to avoid that at all costs. That would be something other people would be able to hear.

Wrestling within herself she briefly took back control. "I couldn't let you do that. I had to be able to give him some comfort, but not so much that he wanted to have a full conversation with you. It's too risky, and I wasn't going to give that madame the op..."

She didn't get to finish the sentence because the spirit took over again and groaned loud enough for Cory to expect the doorknob to rattle at any moment with Flossie trying to enter the room.

"I need you to calm down and get out of me. I cannot have anyone find you here."

"Who cares who finds me? I want to be found. I need to tell my love that things are not good and that he must be careful." She was almost at conversation volume, and this had to be stopped before she started shouting.

"I can relay a message." Cory knew that she would have to do some really fancy footwork to deliver any kind of message to a family she was barely acquainted with regarding a situation she had no hand in, but if it would get the ghost to release her, she was willing to promise almost anything. Almost.

"I want to relay the message." Cory's hand slammed down on the vanity, causing the perfume bottles Ezra had always brought her after every dig to rattle on the shelves on either side of the mirror. Her eyes widened, though she was not the one who had told her body to move in that way.

"No, and you must leave. Now."

"No, I believe I might have figured this out. And in fact, I could deliver that message right now if I was so inclined." The sly smile on her face made Cory even sicker in her stomach. She might not be able to stop herself from going down into the foyer, calling the carriage again, and showing back up to the Havershalls' house. And that could be an absolute doom for her.

She was no madam. She'd never tried to tout herself as one, and she did not want to be sought after to talk to the dead as others were wont to proclaim. In truth, really speaking to the dead could lead them to root in your soul and not let go. And she couldn't have that.

Still, she watched in horror as she rose from the vanity chair, smoothed her hair from her forehead, pulled her gloves back on, and again smiled at herself in the mirror.

"I believe it would be much easier for us to simply take your secret passage than it would be to try to walk through the house. It's so interesting in here..."

Sick to her stomach was an understatement. Cory was going to throw up, and there would be nothing she could do to stop it.

So much for trying to be helpful and give some solace to a man who was grieving. Now she was going to make it even worse by turning up on his doorstep as an older woman with a younger woman's words and attitudes. Probably also information he was not going to be happy with.

They trekked across the floor, and Cory tried one last time to halt their progress by gripping the tied-back curtains. She struggled to hang on for dear life and not let the spirit overtake her, but each of her fingers was methodically pulled from the fabric, and she stumbled as she was jerked away from the window.

Even though she didn't want to, she walked to the closet knowing that the panel behind it could be released to open into the secret passage.

And this was one secret of the house that even Flossie didn't know about.

A knock sounded on her bedroom door behind her, and Flossie called through the stout wood. But when Cory tried to answer her, the spirit clamped down on her vocal cords and pushed her farther into the passage.

This was not the first time that Cory had essentially been possessed. It might not even be the last, but right now it was the most terrifying. Her heart was booming in her chest, her palms were sweaty, and her scalp tingled. She had to come up with a way to get the spirit out, but it would have to be something she didn't think about, just did out of the blue or the spirit might be able to counter her before she had a chance to act.

Dammit! She had known she would pay for helping that grieving man earlier, but this hadn't happened in years. Being possessed was not for the weak-hearted, and it wasn't for the faint of heart either. Cory was neither of those, but this was more powerful than it had ever been before. And she had no way out except to follow along with the one possessing her and hope she came up with something before they got to the Havershalls.

Creeping down the narrow hallway inside the walls of the house Ezra had been so proud of, she tried to think of what she would have wanted to hear him say, how he might have talked with her if he'd come to visit her or if she had called out for him.

The idea had definitely been one she'd entertained when she had been in the police's sights for his death. She'd thought endlessly of bringing Ezra to her not only to say goodbye, but also to see if he knew anything that would help her find the real killer.

But the risk had been too great, and so she'd waited for the information to present itself, for the police to do their job. She wasn't going to have the luxury of doing that this time.

"Listen to me, please. I know you want to talk with your husband, but this is a very bad idea..." She sputtered as the ghost squeezed her throat with her own hand.

"I'm the one talking here. I have to warn him. As much as I love him, I cannot have him join me just yet, he has too much to live for. I'm taking you with me so that we can warn him and then I promise I will consider leaving. He is aware of my abilities with magic but not the consequences it has wrought."

Promise to consider? That was not warming her heart. There was a way to get her out of Cory's body, but Cory didn't want to think about that and certainly not do it. She might not have a choice though.

And if she had magic, then why hadn't she ever told her family that Madam Olivia was a fraud?

That question was abruptly cut off as the possession grew more complete. The hallway ended in a T, and Cory found herself heading to the left to go down the narrow set of stairs at the back of the house. From there they would go down one more set of stairs to another tunnel, this one coming out right at the foot of a tree next to her back garden.

She tried not to think about it too hard, only enough to get them where this woman was determined to go. Her footsteps became jerky on the second set of stairs, and Cory desperately hoped the spirit was weakening. She hated the thought of eradicating her, but there might not be another way.

"It's dank down here," she said. Either of them could have meant the words, but the ghost had been the one to say them.

"Yes, it is. We're underground and we shouldn't be here." Cory choked on the last word but fought hard to get it out.

"We won't be here for long. I have to tell him that his life is in danger. He's been so wrapped up in business that he hasn't seen what damage his partner has been doing. The man is detestable, and is always looking to possess anything that isn't his."

"Like you seem to be possessing me?" Cory shouldn't have said that because it would only incite the ghost more, but she couldn't seem to help herself. What happened to those days when she'd just sit in her study, looking at plants and waiting for it to be dinner time so she and Ezra could compare their work from the day?

"I am not...oh, huh, I guess I am. It won't be for long though, I promise. As soon as I get the message about the dead women to my husband, he can confront this abomination and send him straight to hell for also killing me."

"What dead women?"

But the ghost went silent as they walked up the stairs to the back garden. There was a door in what appeared to be a shed with her gardening tools. Those things did reside in here, but then so did a small bench with rows and rows of deadly dried herbs and this door that would let her pass back and forth between the house and the garden without having to answer any messy questions about what she was doing.

Cory gripped the knob of the door to the shed to prevent them from opening it until she got her answer. "What women? What dead women are you talking about?"

"Whores, which makes me wonder why he killed me too. I couldn't even stand to be with my husband more than once a month. I'm certainly not going to be out on the streets letting just anyone rut at me, I'll have you know."

"Okay, then who was the killer?" Cory lost her grip on the knob and it turned, allowing the door to start its slow swing open. "Who was the killer?"

"I can't..." the other woman faded out and Cory desperately tried to keep her this time instead of sending her away. If she knew what had happened and if she could name who had done it, then there could be justice served. But first she needed a name!

"Who is it?" she nearly yelled as she backed against the long table.

A full shiver ran down her body and she knew she was losing the one who might have the answers.

"I..."

The door swung the rest of the way open and Cory fell chest-first into the last person on earth or elsewhere that she'd want to see right now. Or ever, really.

"Do you often have conversations with yourself and have to pull yourself forcefully away from the window? Or look surprised that you've smacked your hand on a vanity?" Mr. Reardon did not let go of her even as she wiggled to get free and parts of him touched parts of her that should not have lit up like they were on fire inside her.

Damn.

CHAPTER 9

"Do you often find yourself trespassing and spying on unsuspecting women through their bedroom windows?" Coriander pushed against her captor, but Mr. Reardon would not budge. "Unhand me, sir."

It was as if the man were made of stone, which would certainly explain the rocks in his head. How dare he show up at her home unannounced in the middle of the night and traipse through her garden as if he were the rightful owner of Elmcroft?

If she were a lesser witch, she would march back down into her herb cellar and retrieve enough of her foxglove draft to cloud not only Mr. Reardon's memory of her ghostly possession but every one of his memories where she was concerned.

Alas, Cory was a conservative witch who much preferred a fire under her cauldron to one under her feet.

Fear of further exposing her magical talents wasn't the only reason Coriander refrained from using her gifts. Mr. Reardon had been at the scene of the latest murder—a murder very likely connected to Franny's. He knew more than he was letting on. Which meant Cory needed his memories intact.

There was also the spark of attraction to the infuriating man. Which Coriander chalked up to basic physical needs and chose to ignore. Something that became more difficult the longer he held on to her.

"Mr. Reardon." Coriander stomped her boot heel on the top of his foot, scuffing the fine polish of his expensive black leather shoes. "I demand that you release me at once."

"My apologies, Ms. Whitlock." His fingers trailed down her arms as he released her from his grip and took several steps back, putting a polite and acceptable distance between them. "There are pressing matters that I wish to discuss with you."

"Social calls are made after the sun comes up and held in a parlor." She rubbed her hands up and down her arms in an attempt to stop the tingling sensation left behind from his touch.

"Not all social calls, Ms. Whitlock." One corner of his mouth upturned in a wicked grin as he took in Cory's wide eyes and parted lips, obviously relishing her shock at his insinuation. "And I did say they were pressing matters."

"The familiarity in the manner with which you choose to speak to me is more shocking than the implied meaning of your choice of words." Cory grabbed a handful of burgundy silk, raised the hem of her skirt, and pivoted on her boot heel to march back into the house. "I would suggest a calling card for future visits. Good evening, Mr. Reardon."

Coriander had no intentions of entering the house the same way she exited it, opting for a longer, less direct route through the kitchen entrance instead. A silly precaution considering he caught her stumbling out of the garden shed, but it was one she needed to take. It was routine, and in these uncertain times with a murderer on the loose, she took comfort in the small familiarities of safer days spent with Ezra.

"Perhaps I should call on Special Inspector Parker instead." Pea gravel stones crushed underfoot as Mr. Reardon followed her down the garden path that looped around to the side of the house and the kitchen's double-hung door. "He might take an interest in your involvement in tonight's theatrics. Your performance just now has me more convinced of a partnership with Madam Olivia than ever."

If Coriander had a glove on her hand, she would have slipped it off and smacked it across his cheek. She couldn't recall the last time she had been so offended, and given the events of her life over the previous year, that was saying something.

"You cannot honestly believe that I am in any way associated with that charlatan?" She rounded on him but kept her temper and her hands to herself. She would not let an insufferable man like Mr. Reardon get the better of her.

"This is not the first of Madam Olivia's séances that I have attended." He crossed his arms over his chest, flexed muscles straining the seams along the sleeves of his wool coat.

"I wouldn't have thought you so *enlightened* as to believe in spiritualists and mediums, Mr. Reardon." She allowed her disdain for the frauds masquerading as true mystics to seep through her words, hoping to convince him that she had nothing to do with the madam.

The sooner she threw him off of her use of magic, the sooner he would leave. Cory didn't have time for this man or Special Inspector Parker to poke around in her private affairs. Not when she needed to follow a new lead in her investigation into Franny's death—the late Mrs. Havershall. Any connection between the death of a member of the ton and the apparent homicides of a witch and a so-called fallen woman was worth researching further.

"I believe what I can see with my own eyes." His gaze narrowed as if taking her weight and measure. "And what I saw this evening was most intriguing. As I said, I've attended my share of Madam Olivia's séances and they are nothing if not predictable. Just smoke and mirrors, in my professional opinion."

"Your professional opinion? And what profession might that be?" Coriander had a sinking feeling she knew precisely what it was that Mr. Reardon did to earn his living.

"Let's not be coy with one another, Ms. Whitlock. You are aware of the organization with which I am employed. Just as I am aware that the only difference between this evening's séance and the others Madam Olivia has performed was you." A small silver pin fastened to the lapel of his coat bearing the insignia of the Society of Paraphysical Research glinted in the moonlight. "Ms. Whitlock, you're shivering. Perhaps you would prefer to discuss this further with a cup of hot tea and the warmth of your fireplace?"

"I would prefer it if you would leave." Coriander rested her hands on her hips and held her ground between the kitchen door and Mr. Reardon.

"A cup of tea and a few moments of your time and then I'll be on my way." Mr. Reardon made a point to invade her personal space as he strode by her and opened the door to the kitchen. "After you."

Magic coursed through her veins and crackled at her fingertips as she elbowed her way past Mr. Reardon and into her kitchen. It took everything she had to swallow her temper along with her powers, all but choking on the magic as she reigned herself in. Coriander was wound tighter than the cogs in her departed husband's failed inventions. If Mr. Reardon continued to push her, Cory would not be held responsible for her actions. She almost wanted to hold him in the kitchen long enough to have the machine that threw knives come to life.

And a little dose of her foxglove memory draft would see that she wasn't held accountable.

Coriander lit a fire in the stove and busied herself with preparing the tea while Mr. Reardon settled into a chair at the small wooden table in the center of the room. The sooner he drank his cup and asked his questions, the sooner he would be off. The sun was cresting over the horizon, ushering in a new day and with it eventually her cousin in search of a hot breakfast. The last thing she needed was for Flossie to discover her alone with a man—especially one under the employ of the SPR.

"Ask your questions, Mr. Reardon." Coriander added steeped tea to a porcelain pot, stacked a pair of matching cups, and set everything on the table. "I'll do my best to answer them, though I know little of Madam Olivia beyond the séance at the Havershalls'."

"I'm inclined to believe you as I have not seen you at any of her other gatherings." Mr. Reardon reached for the pot and poured the steaming amber liquid into both teacups.

"*How kind of you.*" Coriander bit her tongue to keep from saying something she would regret and wrapped her hands around the porcelain, absorbing the warmth from the hot liquid and the aroma of cinnamon, cloves, and orange rind.

Mr. Reardon pulled a small silver flask from the inner pocket of his jacket and added a splash of spirits to his cup. "You may not think me kind by the end of our conversation, Ms. Whitlock, but I assure you these questions are absolutely necess..."

The paranormal investigator trailed off as his attention was pulled elsewhere. One of Ezra's confounded inventions chugged and whirred into the kitchen with its dustpan and broom at the ready in an attempt to sweep the hardwood floors. It left a trail of dirt in its wake as it made its way across the kitchen and out the servants' entrance into the parlor.

"My husband was an inventor of sorts," Coriander answered the question before Mr. Reardon had the opportunity to ask it.

"Is that so?" He swiveled in his seat, watching the backend of Ezra's steam-powered cleaner as it disappeared out into the hall. "I'd heard he was somewhat of an adventurer, caught the Egypt bug, hitched up with a group of archaeologists, and headed off into the desert."

"He was a scientist." She narrowed her gaze, peering at Mr. Reardon over the rim of her cup. Adventurer was an acceptable term for her husband's work, and yet, she took offense and felt compelled to defend her husband's memory. "His current field of study involved the marvels and mysteries of Egyptian engineering and the construction of the pyramids."

Mr. Reardon had the decency to appear chagrined and apologized for the unintentional slight against her husband's memory.

"You didn't trespass in my garden to discuss my husband, Mr. Reardon." Coriander reached for the teapot and topped off her cup.

"No, I didn't." He turned in his chair, took a sip of his liquor-infused tea and refocused his attention on Coriander. "You've said you were not previously acquainted with Madam Olivia and while I believe you, I am struck by the coincidence of your presence at her first successful conversation with the dead. Almost as much as I was to find you at the scene of a murder."

"If there was a question in there, Mr. Reardon, I failed to hear it." Coriander drained the last of her tea, set her cup on the table, and folded her hands in her lap.

"Are you aware of the connection between the deceased?" Mr. Reardon's sharp gaze searched her face for any telltale signs that she was withholding information, but she remained stoic under the scrutiny and hid her shock that he may hold the key to the late Mrs. Havershall's ties to the other victims. "Katherine and Franny were more than roommates, Ms. Whitlock."

"Do you mean to imply they were lovers?" Coriander hid her disappointment over the lack of information about Mrs. Havershall behind a mask of shock at the perceived scandal. Her friend's romantic preferences were of no consequence to her, but they were a useful distraction from the line of questions she feared would follow.

"What?" Mr. Reardon sputtered, choking on a mouthful of tea. "Of course not. Don't be ridiculous. The reason I'm here has nothing to do with whom they shared their bed, but the magical knowledge your friend Franny shared with her roommate."

"Now who is the ridiculous one?" Coriander scoffed in an effort to dissuade his belief that Franny was a practitioner of the craft. "Magic doesn't exist any more than leprechauns or werewolves do."

"Until this investigation, I would have been in agreement with you. To my utter horror, the deeper I dig, the more evidence I find to the contrary." He unscrewed the top to his flask and added another splash of what smelled like whiskey to his tea.

"Forgive my confusion, Mr. Reardon. You say that you were a skeptic." Coriander arched her brow and tilted her head to one side as she studied the man across from her. "You also mentioned that you are under the employ of the Society of Paraphysical Research. I've read about them in The Times and wasn't aware they accepted nonbelievers amongst their ranks."

"The most thorough investigations are done with a skeptical mind, Ms. Whitlock." He raised his teacup to his lips, hesitated to take a sip, and set it back on the table before exchanging it for the flask of whiskey. "At least that's what I used to believe."

"And now?" she asked, both intrigued and terrified by what his answer might be.

"I find myself tumbling down Alice's rabbit hole." Mr. Reardon recapped his flask and stuffed it back into his coat pocket. "Your friend was a witch, Ms. Whitlock, and I suspect you knew that because before you found safety and security inside the walls of Elmcroft, you practiced the arts with her."

"I have been accused of many things in my life, Mr. Reardon, but this is a first." Coriander pushed her chair back from the table and rose to her feet. "As entertaining as this conversation has been, I think it's time for you to leave."

She marched across the kitchen and pulled open the double-hung door with more force than necessary

"Please, I've heard the rumors," he jeered, attempting to antagonize her further as he stood from the table and followed her to the door. He closed the distance between them and leaned in, his mouth a hairsbreadth from hers. The decadent combination of whiskey and tea on his breath was somehow intoxicating—and yet had nothing to do with the alcohol content. "I've had a glimpse of your world, Ms. Whitlock. I will ferret out the truth about the nature of your magic and your will to use it and present my findings to the SPR."

"Good evening, Mr. Reardon." Coriander motioned toward the door. "Please see yourself out."

"It seems I have overstayed my welcome." Mr. Reardon stepped out onto the pea-gravel path, pausing before he reached the curve towards the back of the house. "I'll call on you again. Soon."

"Is that a threat, sir?" Coriander leaned against the door jamb and crossed her arms over her chest.

"It's a promise." He turned on his heel, grinding the small stones beneath his boot, and marched down the path.

She watched him go until he disappeared from sight and she felt certain he wouldn't return. At least for the time being.

After her possession by the late Mrs. Havershall and the taxing visit from Mr. Reardon, Coriander was exhausted and wanted nothing more than to crawl into bed.

With the paranormal investigator's threat looming over her head, sleep eluded her. Her thoughts were plagued by the infuriating Mr. Reardon and the possibility of an SPR inquisition into her magic. Coriander knew beyond a reasonable doubt that she hadn't seen the last of him.

Mr. Reardon promised to return, and she was under the impression that he was a man who kept his promises.

CHAPTER 10

"You didn't!" Flossie grabbed another scone and shoved it in her mouth.

Cory barely sustained the urge to roll her eyes at her cousin. "Of course I did, but I also did it in the best possible way. I can't have him calling here at all hours of the night. That's not only unseemly, it's inconvenient, especially since I'll be harvesting this weekend, and I need to continue with my research. Something has to clue me in to what happened, Flossie. It must!"

"But you'll be playing with fire if you take this on. He seems very astute, and while I know you are very smart, you sometimes lack...hmmm, how do I want to say this? You lack common sense and the ability to hide in plain sight, dear cousin."

"I do not!" Cory grabbed the pot of steaming-hot tea the cook had placed on the table and splashed some into her cup from the night before. It sloshed out the side and hit her wrist, scalding the flesh. "Damn."

"Language, Cory, language!" Flossie quirked an eyebrow at Cory, but Cory ignored her as best she could.

The sting smarted, but she was not going to tell her cousin that. Apparently, Flossie was too busy judging her on things she knew nothing about.

Reaching a hand across the table, Flossie picked up one of the cloth napkins, dipped it in the glass of ice to her left, and placed it on Cory's red skin. "Maybe not common sense, perhaps that's too harsh. But you do have to admit that for most of your life you hid out here, or behind Ezra. You did not navigate this on your own, and without him here I just wonder if you're taking on too much. There will be no one to shield you if you get caught up with a murderer who wants their secret kept at all costs."

She was not wrong but Cory had to do this. She could not let the injustice and the pure evil of a murderer go unpunished, especially if she could find clues to help and was able to put her friend to rest. Mr. Reardon was high on her list of people to consider.

She told Flossie as much and the insufferable woman banged her forehead onto the dining table, hard enough to make the tea saucers jump.

Esther rushed in to see if something was wrong, but Cory waved her off after pointing at Flossie and winking at her.

"Please calm yourself or I might need to call the authorities. We'll see if Special Inspector Parker needs to ask you a few questions."

Flossie lifted her head so quickly Cory was afraid she might tip backward in her chair. "You wouldn't!"

"I think we've already established that I can and I would do many things. That inability to have common sense, I suppose."

"Now, Coriander, let's not get ahead of ourselves here. I simply meant that you had a shield, and a formidable one at that, in Ezra. You rarely had to deal with outsiders, you spent most of your time in this house or in your garden. He made that possible for you from a young age. You and he walked right into a marriage that didn't force you to twirl and flitter for the ton for some man to notice you. So yes, you don't always know the restrictions of society, and you don't always follow the rules. That hasn't gotten you into too much trouble before now. But we need to be careful. You can't just traipse off into the middle of an investigation simply because you don't like the answers you're getting."

"I'm not an imbecile, I do know what I can and cannot do." Inside, she wasn't as confident of those words as she sounded on the outside, but she'd be damned before she admitted it.

Flossie slapped a hand over her face and was obviously at her wit's end. But then so was Cory. An impasse of sorts.

"You have a caller, miss." Esther stood at the threshold of the dining room with her hands clasped in front of her chest and a worried look on her normally jovial face.

What now?

"As you can see, we're in the midst of breakfast, Esther. Perhaps they could come back another time. Have them leave their card." The last thing she wanted right now was to talk to anyone else. Although that did sort of prove Flossie's point. Of course, Cory would never admit that out loud.

"It's the patriarch of the Havershall family, ma'am. Are you sure you want me to send him away?"

Flossie's hand immediately went to her hair, and then she smoothed down the front of her morning dress. For her part Cory rolled her eyes. If she kept that up, she was going to give herself a headache.

There was no way out of this, even she knew that. Her conscience, her belief in justice, and her desire to lay her friend to complete rest wouldn't let her quit.

"Please have him wait in the front parlor. With the early hour, I'm afraid I'm not quite presentable yet."

"No need to make yourself any prettier for me, dear heart. Are those pasties? Oh, I would kill for one of those. The Mrs. has me on a strict diet and so I never get sweets anymore, just ham and eggs."

One of the highest-ranking men of the ton pulled out the chair next to Cory and planted himself there as if he had no intention of leaving anytime soon.

Esther shrugged her shoulders and winced.

"More tea please, Esther. Perhaps some more of your delightful scones with that strawberry cream." Cory raised an eyebrow at Esther, who nodded. Hopefully she'd gotten the message Cory was trying to transmit. A little Valerian root to make him complacent could go a long way toward getting away with not revealing anything depending on what he was doing here. She wouldn't serve it until she found out what he wanted, but being ready was forever at the forefront of her mind after the way she'd been treated during Ezra's murder investigation.

"It's a pleasure to see you again so soon, my lord," Cory said.

"Of course it is, madam, I live only to entertain." He waved Esther out of the room with a regal gesture and as soon as she left, he leaned in, fully in Cory's personal space. "Can we trust the one across the table?" he asked in a hushed voice.

Cory sat back as far in her chair as she could, but there was no escaping him. For every inch she crept back he leaned forward until finally there was nowhere to go.

"Yes, this is my cousin Floss…Florence. She was with me last night at the séance."

"Séance my ass." He grabbed another pasty and took multiple bites before popping the last morsel into his big mouth. "I was expecting it to just be more of that woo woo kind of stuff but something was different last night. I let my wife have those damned things in an effort to keep her busy but last night was real. I know it, and since you were the only one who'd never been there before, I wondered if you had some insight into why that is."

Cory made every effort not to look at Flossie because she knew her cousin would be either glaring at her or smirking, and Cory needed neither.

"I'm sorry, my lord, but I don't know why it was different. Whatever Madam Olivia was able to do was all on her own. I'm not sure that I even believe in that kind of spirituality." She was very proud of herself for not choking on that last word. Sham was what it was, truth be told, not any kind of spirituality, but she certainly was not about to get into an argument with this man who had just shoved yet one more scone into her tea and was swirling it around.

He pointed a finger at her that was dripping with jam and winked. "Ah, I understand. Of course, you can't admit anything or you'd get hung, is that correct? Or do they still burn witches at the stake?" He laughed but it came out as anything but mirth. "I'll tell you what, it'll be our little secret if you come to the opera tonight. I have someone I'd like you to meet."

"Unfortunately, Florence and I already have plans—"

But he cut her off. "That wasn't a request, dear heart. Eight o'clock tonight at the opera. Wear something that's a little more, how should I say this? Tantalizing. Yes, I believe that's the word I'm looking for." He winked again. "The man you're meeting will expect a bit of a show before he answers any of your questions, but I want to know if he's lying or if he really can talk to the dead. You'll do this for me, won't you? I have a feeling it might just be worth your life to arrive promptly at eight." Glancing over at Flossie, he took his time eyeing her then said, "Alone." He took the last scone and dropped it in Cory's tea, splashing the liquid on the front of her morning dress.

Esther came in through the door as he saw himself out. Her hands were frantically rubbing over each other like she was trying to wash them clean without water.

As if that action finally broke the panic keeping Cory anchored to her chair, she shot up and raced to the front door just in time to see him ride off on a horse. He turned and flipped a wave to her as if they'd just had a delightful talk about the weather and what the crown was doing, not him threatening her life.

Flossie gently removed her fingers from around the edge of the door. She'd dug in almost to the point of gouging the old wood.

"We can do this, Cory. Don't let him freak you out. He has no proof and no way of showing what he doesn't have. Don't let him get under your skin. You're tougher than this. I'll go with you, and we'll show them who not to mess with. No magic, nothing but us and our very smart brains."

"You mean the one I have that seems to lack common sense?" Flossie had pried her last finger from the door and took her fist in her hand.

"We don't need common sense here. We're going to have to wing it in a very serious situation or risk everything. But perhaps we can get enough answers for you that you can finally leave this alone as I've been asking you to do. We have an opportunity to show his lord that we have nothing to do with any of this."

"He said I have to go alone. You heard him."

"Yes, but how will he—"

"You truly think he won't stop you or won't care if he can prove something or not before he throws it out into the gossip mill? Look at what happened when people thought I was a murderer, Flossie. Being a witch would actually somehow be worse. If we're going to play along, then we need to play along all the way or risk exposure."

She knew what she said made sense, and eventually Flossie agreed with her even though she did it very grudgingly. But inside Cory was shaking. On the outside, though, she held herself as still and calm as she had when the letter had come telling her of her husband's death and even when the constable had come around to accuse her of being the one who'd had him killed. As it had then, the posture only lasted until the door was shut and then she broke, sinking to the floor, not sure what she was going to do.

"Fine, you're going to the opera," Flossie said, pulling Cory up by her hand. "No if, ands, or buts. You can do this. And then maybe you'll let it go. Just don't say anything you shouldn't and leave every single trick here except an amulet for protection. We can pin it to your dress as an accessory. Esther, can you fetch the one? We have little time to get everything in place."

Many hours later, Cory found herself being ushered into the grand theater in Covent Garden. The doormen bowed as she walked through the entrance, and she was immediately escorted to a box on the third level. She wished Flossie was here so she could grip her hand, but she was alone, just as Havershall had told her to be.

Long ago, Ezra had tried to get her interested in the opera, but there was little for her here other than the music that could help flowers grow. The pomp and circumstance of having to sit in an area with all these people, enclosed and not able to move much beyond the box, had never been her strong suit or her desire. Ezra would sometimes come alone, but that was mainly to use a device he'd been tinkering with to record voices and songs to then listen to again at home. He'd tried to explain it to her, but she'd never quite understood what it was. She heard plenty of voices that weren't hers throughout the day, she'd felt no need to add to that.

She had, however, remembered the device and that Ezra had been particularly proud of how it caught the slightest sounds even if it was nestled in a pocket as it currently was in her frock. She'd bypassed the amulet Flossie had wanted her to wear and chose this as protection instead

She had donned a black dress this evening against Flossie's wishes. Fading into the background was exactly what she wanted to do and the faster she met this man, whoever he was, and got what information she needed, the faster she could sneak out of the darkened theater while people stared raptly at the stage.

At least that's what she hoped for.

Until it was almost intermission and she saw the man coming up the balcony toward her. Timothy Revelson, Ezra's former best friend, the man who'd killed her husband and should have been in jail, smiled at her as he entered the box and sat across from her.

"Darling Coriander, I'm sorry we had to meet like this, but I certainly do appreciate you coming out on such short notice. I know how you hate to be in public, but I thought it would be bad form to show up at your house unannounced after my release."

CHAPTER 11

"Your release." Coriander drew out the words, peeled her black satin evening gloves from her hands and gripped them tight, imaging Mr. Revelson's neck in their place.

Her lips mashed into a thin line as she gathered her wits and her fury. It would not do to lose her temper or her magic within the walls of the opera house. Though a few drops of her delirium draft into his brandy was a tempting idea. While not as satisfying as the cold, dank cells in Newgate prison, a straight-waistcoat and a room at Bedlam would suffice.

If she'd only thought to bring some of it with her.

Of course, there was no way for her to know the man Lord Havershall wanted her to speak with would be the man responsible, convicted and incarcerated for dear Ezra's death. What did he stand to gain from arranging this meeting? Why did Havershall say he could speak to the dead and wanted to know if that was a lie? Was Havershall also involved in her husband's untimely demise or was Revelson holding something over the old lord's head? While she suspected the latter, she could not rule out the former. The senior Havershall's part in all this was yet another puzzle to piece together.

One that would have to wait until her meeting with the repugnant Revelson concluded. Preferably with a strong pot of tea and a stiff drink.

The image of Larkin Reardon and his silver flask flashed in her mind, and she couldn't help but think his opinion of her would only lessen if he were to see her in Havershall's box with Revelson. Charlatans and prostitutes were not enough. She could now add murderers to the list of social callers.

Not that it mattered what he thought of her or the company she kept.

"Perhaps you could explain to me how this came about?" Cory pushed thoughts of one infuriating man from her mind and focused on another seated right in front of her as she stood. "Has the magistrate had a change of heart or mind that I am not aware of?"

"Of a sorts. Assuming you provide the proof I require to clear my name." Timothy slipped his hand beneath the lapel of his black tailcoat, his fingers dipping into the small pocket of the matching waistcoat. He arched a bushy brow over widened eyes at the sharp end of Cory's broach pointed in his face. "No cause for alarm, Coriander dear. Or violence."

Timothy removed an intricately engraved pocket watch from the small pocket of his black satin waistcoat and pressed the small button to release the case front, revealing the face. Coriander was familiar with the timepiece. In fact, its twin had rested on the dressing table in her bedroom until that very evening where it now resided in her reticule. As far as she knew it did not have the same mechanisms hers had, but just seeing it made her eyes well up. The watch had been a gift from Ezra to Timothy celebrating their latest archaeological endeavor. A small treasure in her husband's eyes, one he'd gifted to someone who he thought was his best friend and instead was his killer. It was the kiss of Judas as far as Coriander was concerned.

"Time is short, Coriander." He snapped the case front closed with the flick of his wrist, returned the watch to his pocket, and motioned to the red and gold velvet chair beside him. "I need evidence to prove my innocence in our beloved Ezra's death. A name to clear my own. And you are going to help me get it. Now, take a seat. It is of the utmost importance that you hear what I have to say."

"You believe everything you have to say is of the utmost importance. It has always been one of your least appealing qualities." Coriander tucked her gloves inside her reticule and felt for the pocket watch's stem wind, turning it twice in a counterclockwise direction. Removing her hand from her bag, she crossed her arms in front of her waist, refused to sit and offered her best glare. "That and your capability for murder. Why would I help you?"

"Because your relentless pursuit of justice for Ezra led to my being convicted. Wrongly convicted, I might add." Timothy pressed the toe of his boot against the chair leg, pushing it closer to Coriander. "If not for my testimony, I would have swung from the gallows."

"Oh? You mean, the same way your lies led to my being accused of killing my husband and under the watchful eye of Special Inspector Parker as his first suspect?" Cory remained standing, her right foot tapping a rhythm with the intensity of the percussion in the orchestra pit below.

"Yes, well." Timothy waved his hand and tilted his head in deference to Coriander. "You were more likely to have done it than me and as a woman would have received less of a sentence. They could have assumed it was an accident and let you keep to your little gardening life out in the country. Isn't that always what you wanted? That's what Ezra was completely convinced of. It could have been a gift of sorts to leave you without any suitors or a reputation to keep up if you look at it correctly."

"If you think that ridiculous thought will help your case with me, you are mistaken." Cory was done with formalities, refusing to address him as sir or any other title. "The only help you will receive from me is acquiring an escort back to Newgate."

"Coriander, please. Do you want me to beg?" Timothy pushed from his seat and fell to his knees on the floor before her with his hands clasped together as if he were in fervent prayer. "Fine, I'll beg."

"Mr. Revelson, compose yourself." Coriander all but hissed at the man, glancing around the theater to ensure no one saw them. An elderly couple in a box opposite theirs trained their spectacles on Cory, only to avert their attention back to the opera when she craned her head in their direction. "You're embarrassing me and humiliating yourself with this futile display."

"But you must help, Cory." Timothy grabbed hold of her skirt, balling the fine silk fabric up in his palms. "My life depends upon it."

"Your life depends on whether or not you unhand Ms. Whitlock." Mr. Reardon, who was unreasonably attractive in his top hat and tailcoat, stormed into the small private balcony box and loomed over Timothy.

In his shock over the invasion, Timothy used the bulk of Coriander's skirt to hoist himself to his feet, threatening the delicate stitching and the tenuous balance she held in her heels. She rocked backward once released, her hip colliding with the rail, and would have toppled over the side if not for Mr. Reardon's quick reflexes. He reached out, clasped his hand around her wrist, and tugged her to his side before any of the audience members were aware of the calamity happening around them.

Perhaps it was the height of the balcony, or the laces of her corset, but she found the air thin and difficult to breathe. Her chest heaved against the confines of the fitted bodice with each attempt to fill her lungs, her heart battering itself against her ribcage. She'd almost fallen to her death and no amount of magic would have spared her from that. Mr. Reardon had saved her life.

And now she was in his debt.

"Are you all right, Coriander?" Larkin turned his back on Revelson and scrutinized every inch of her, surveying her person for injury. "Has he harmed you?"

"Are you following me, Mr. Reardon?" Coriander arched her brow, her mouth curved with a challenging smile as she tried to fake her way through how horribly this whole night had gone awry.

"Hardly, Ms. Whitlock." Larkin's devilish smile combined with the glint in his whiskey-brown eyes said otherwise. "I happened to procure two tickets for the opera this evening. Imagine my surprise to find myself seated in the next box."

"A fortunate coincidence." Caught in his gaze, she surveyed his handsome features, the hard line of his jaw, straight line of his nose both softened by the gas lamps fixed to the wall on either side of the box.

"Indeed." Larkin continued to admire her the way a cat might admire a bowl of its favorite cream.

The rough sound of Timothy clearing his throat freed her from Larkin's thrall and drew her attention from her problematic rescuer to the original problem before her.

"Mr. Reardon, is it?" Timothy straightened his dress shirt and tugged the hem of his waistcoat, regaining his composure along with his footing. "I don't believe I've had the pleasure of making your acquaintance."

He extended his hand in a more formal and customary introduction than the one made while on his knees. Larkin banked the heat in his eyes, and the flecks of gold that mesmerized Cory all but disappeared in the stone-cold look he fixed upon Timothy.

"I have enough acquaintances." Larkin turned to Cory, tucked his chin, and tipped his hat. "Ms. Whitlock."

The spring of tension coiled between them had been released, putting an end to another fleeting moment of attraction—an attraction that seemed to build whenever she was around Larkin Reardon—and she was grateful for the reprieve. Nothing good could come of drawing more of his attention to herself.

The silver pin on his lapel was proof enough of that.

"Mr. Reardon." Cory's squared shoulders, straight spine, and raised chin were dismissal enough for the SPR investigator, who saw his way out of the private box without another word.

Still, she suspected Larkin would seek her out before the night, or the opera, was over. She intended to disappear into the crowd during intermission and slip out before they had another *chance* encounter.

"Interesting company you keep." Timothy watched the heavy velvet curtain as if waiting for a hand to draw it back and reveal another surprise.

"I might have said the same of my husband." If looks could kill, there would have been daggers in Cory's eyes. "If he were still alive."

"Cory, you're not listening to me. I've already said I'm innocent of Ezra's death." Timothy dropped down into his seat and crossed one leg over the other, his foot bobbing up and down. "There was another man involved in our trip to Egypt. I never knew his name, or at least not his real name. He was a partner, financier of sorts."

"Financier?"

This was the first she'd heard of another business associate. It was unlike Ezra to involve outsiders in his work or his finances. Until his last venture through the Suez Canal, his accounts were more than adequate to fund his travels—and his inventions. And then it clicked.

"Please tell me your gambling debts are not responsible for Ezra's death?" Cory's mind reeled and stomach roiled with the possibility that Revelson's overindulgence with alcohol, opium and cards was the catalyst for her husband's murder.

"I thought he wanted a share of the riches. Gold, jewels, that sort of thing." Timothy planted both feet on the floor, rested his elbows on his knees, and leaned forward. "But it was a different sort of treasure my associate was after. The same one Ezra had been after. I didn't know. I swear to you, Cory, I didn't know. The man, he bought my debts, you see."

"And did he find what he was searching for in the sand, Timothy?"

Coriander was shocked to realize that she believed him, but the truth of his confession rang in her ears and resonated in her heart. The more people she spoke with, the more questions she had. Who was this mystery financier? How was Lord Havershall, one of London's most upstanding citizens, involved? How and why was she at the center of so much death? It was as if Cheron had relocated his soul-ferrying business from the river Styx to banks of the Thames.

"And what part does Lord Havershall have to play in all this?" The cogs and gears within her mind began to turn with yet another puzzle and murder to solve. One that should have been solved with Timothy's conviction. "Why would a man of his status reduce himself to playing the role of messenger for a drunken gambler? What does he know?"

What she wanted to ask was how Havershall knew she was a witch. But there was no way to know for certain if Timothy knew. Unless, of course, he told her.

"He knows a great many things." Timothy stared at the floor, as if the mysteries of the universe would be revealed in the grain of the wooden planks. "As do I.

Including some of your, shall we say, out of the ordinary proclivities..."

Coriander wanted nothing more than to give Timothy a piece of her mind and a taste of her magic but held her tongue—and her powers. It was best to let him play his hand and share what secrets he thought he knew before she gave too many of her own away. It was bad enough that Larkin and Havershall were onto her and closing in like a pair of Her Majesty's finest hounds on the hunt.

And the Goddess help her when her cousin found out that not one, or two, but three men suspected she was a witch. There wouldn't be enough tea or scones in all of England to soothe that woman once Coriander shared that bit of news.

"Ezra was quite the conversationalist. Especially when he drank." Timothy seemed to be watching for cracks in Coriander's stoney facade. He must have found one because a confident smirk settled on his face. He leaned back in his seat, folded his arms over his chest, and stretched his legs out, crossing them at the ankles. "Don't be disappointed in him, Cory. The nights in Egypt were long and lonesome. He spoke of you often and fondly. It was never his intention to share your secrets. He never forgave himself for revealing what you are."

"And what exactly am I?" Fear gripped her heart and spiked the magic contained within her.

She wanted to unleash herself, to let the energy flow through and out of her body like the conduit that she was. It would be all too easy to draw on that raw power, let it flow wild and free, consuming Timothy and protecting her secret. But with Larkin occupying a nearby booth, the risk was far too great. It was bad enough the investigator was no doubt collecting the confirmation he needed by eavesdropping on a private conversation.

"A witch, Cory." Timothy raised his brows and widened his eyes, as if daring her to deny it.

"You are very bold, or very stupid, Mr. Revelson." Coriander took pleasure in catching Timothy off guard with her sharp retort. "If I am what you say, a witch with powerful magic at her disposal, it doesn't seem all that wise to confront me on your own in a private box with no one to come to your aid."

"Help me find him, Coriander. Help me find the man who framed us both for Ezra's murder, and I will keep your secret."

"My assistance for your silence?" Coriander retrieved her gloves from her reticule and slipped them on, fastening the black pearl buttons at her wrists.

"Find the financier, clear my name, and I will take that secret to my grave, Coriander. You have my word." Timothy pulled the white silk handkerchief from his tailcoat and dabbed his brow.

His word was less than worthless as far as Coriander was concerned, but his terms were agreeable and a win-win scenario for her. She wanted to find this financier as much if not more than Timothy did.

"Double-cross me, Mr. Revelson, and you may find yourself with a bell tied around your finger, six feet under the grass sooner than you think."

It was an idle threat, but Timothy recoiled as she passed, as if she could strike him dead with nothing more than a touch of her hand. If it were that easy, she might have succumbed to the dark arts years ago. As it was, murder with magic was almost as bloody as it was without it.

And Coriander never much cared for the sight of blood, or the idea of spilling it.

Still, a little fear where Timothy Revelson was concerned went a long way. She couldn't afford for him to have the upper hand or to be under his thumb. Their agreement teetered on the edge of blackmail. As did Lord Havershall's so-called *favor*.

The sooner she found this financier, the sooner Ezra would be at peace, and she would be rid of them and free to investigate the other murders.

CHAPTER 12

As Cory left the box, her mind was awhirl with all the possibilities and the consequences of what had just been laid at her feet. She did not want to work with Timothy. In any capacity. And yet if he had not killed Ezra and was telling the truth about the financier, then there was a killer loose who desperately needed to be brought to justice.

Damn!

She stumbled on the hem of her dress as the heavy curtain fell closed behind her, leaving Revelson with the question of whether or not she would hold up her end of the bargain they'd just struck. Not wanting to hit the wall or make another spectacle of herself in the dim corridor she was in, Cory leaned into the stumble and expected to rest softly against the wood separating the boxes.

Instead, she found herself falling through the curtain next door and right into Larkin Reardon's lap.

Scrambling was not going to help her, and wishing the floor would open up and swallow her whole would not happen either. But how to get out of this predicament? Especially since the damage Timothy had done to her skirts to create the stumble in the first place had now ripped a seam altogether, and the dress had a hole right at her waist.

Damn and blast!

For Larkin's part he did not jump up and dump her to the ground or yell in surprise. He didn't even gasp, which she was thankful for. Instead, he merely rose, taking her with him, and then gently pushed a hand under her arm to right her without a single word uttered. He then guided her into his chair and took the one across from her.

"I thought you had two tickets?" she asked. A completely asinine question, but perhaps it would divert him from asking any questions of his own. "I don't want to be here when your companion returns."

His smile sent a warmth through her that should have been a blush but instead felt like an inferno straight from a blazing bonfire.

"I did secure two tickets, but I did not bring anyone with me. You're safe for the moment, and it might be best to let things settle down before you go traipsing off to wherever you were heading before you stumbled."

She placed her reticule on her lap to cover the rip in her dress and wished fervently that she could be anywhere but here. Well anywhere but here as long as it wasn't the box next door with that cretin.

"I did not..." But she trailed off because there was a commotion next door that she couldn't see but could hear.

"Get your hands off me." That was Timothy. Even though his words were muffled, she knew his voice and could hear not only the anger but also a morsel of fear in the words.

Something else was said by another person but the words were lost, and only the gruff tone came through the heavy fabric.

"Unhand me!" That was much louder and followed by scuffling noises. Everything was overlaid by the crescendo of the opera being performed below. When she glanced over the railing, no one was looking up to see what was happening. And when she glanced to the right and across the expanse of the theater, not a single person was looking anywhere but at the stage.

To be fair, there was a soprano on stage with her mouth wide open singing a particularly high note with everything she had in her, and the orchestra in the pit was full of cymbals and drums and horns making enough noise to drown out a street brawl of a hundred men, so it was not surprising.

But then everything went silent in the next box. Larkin raised his eyebrow at Cory as if he wanted to see what her reaction would be, so she sat very still and kept her reticule in her lap. Perhaps he hadn't heard anything. She was the one with her back to the adjoining wall and it was possible with the cacophony going on that he had missed the commotion. Should she say something? Ask if he was the reason Timothy had been accosted in Lord Havershall's box? And what he was being accosted for?

The soprano had ended with a flourish and so had the first act. The theater lights came up and people began milling around the floor, talking excitedly about any number of things. The atmosphere in this box, though, remained as silent as midnight on a moonless night.

"Shall I escort you home? I have a carriage out front that I just need to call around if you don't mind waiting a few moments. You can use my jacket to hide the tear in your dress if you'd rather not have to move through the crowds and explain yourself to anyone."

His offer was not only generous, it was also very conscientious of her predicament and made her realize he knew more than he let on or that she was bad at hiding things.

She had not brought her own carriage and did not want to have Lord Havershall take her back to her home. She didn't know what he knew and wasn't certain if he would have some pointed questions after her meeting with the man who had been convicted of killing her husband.

The question of what they knew for certain regarding her personal life hung in her head too. What would they tell and who would they tell it to?

Larkin was still watching her from his seat. She couldn't afford to continue to put him off. There were only a handful of seconds to come up with how to handle this new wrinkle in her life without showing her hand. She foresaw some serious scrying this evening and if that meant she was up until dawn again, then so be it.

"If you could take me home, I would very much appreciate it." She decided to go with the slight damsel in distress. She could play to what he had saved her from in the next box, instead of the indignation and the absolute resolution brewing in her blood to find her husband's killer and yet still not completely let Timothy off the hook. He had put her husband in danger. He had racked up the debts that had gotten Ezra killed. While he might not have been the one to pour the poison into Ezra's drink, he was still very much the reason the poison was even present at a dig that Ezra had been after for years.

He had to pay for that. Had to.

"If you're ready to go now, we can be on our way. Perhaps it would be best if you came with me to call the coach. I don't think leaving you here alone is in your best interest."

When had they gone from flirting and joking to this serious man trying to take care of her? Then again, it could just be in his normal nature and not something specifically for her. He also had saved her from falling over the balcony and to her death on the floor of an opera house, so there was that to consider.

"I'll go with you. I think I've had enough drama for the evening." Although she knew for certain that the second she stepped in the door at her home, drama would probably be completely unavoidable.

Larkin waited like a gentleman until she'd opened her front door and turned back around to wave before the carriage took off down the lane. She stood in her doorway for a few more seconds trying to figure out how she could avoid seeing Flossie at all and sneak upstairs to begin the work she knew she needed to do. This was no longer a query into what had happened to a long-ago friend. It was no longer a bit of sleuthing to find out who was killing people who were in some way connected to her. This had become personal, and it would end before any other lives were taken.

She made it to her room by the back stairs. Holding her skirt in her hand, she took her shoes off at the bottom of the staircase and tread lightly to the room in the attic, avoiding even Esther when she heard her open a door on the second floor and peek her head out. Cory had work to do and did not want to be interrupted.

As quietly as possible she placed her shoes on the floorboards of the old attic room filled with Ezra's many inventions. She could have cleaned them out months ago, but she had no idea where she'd send them and did not want to lose the reminders of her husband. There were so many things here that represented times of their lives that were both wonderful and frustrating, filled with joy and deep remorse for what could have been if he'd continued to live and hadn't gotten mixed up with that horrible man, Timothy.

She needed to clear her head before she sat down to do any kind of magic, or chaos would ensue and create noise she was not willing to answer for at this time. Turning from the door, she groped along the wall for the light fixture Ezra had created to pull energy from the sun and use it to illuminate the small space. She never could understand exactly how it worked but was thankful for it now.

Or at least she would have been grateful for it if it didn't throw light on the one person she had hoped to avoid the most.

"So, Timothy Revelson joined you in the Havershall box this evening at the opera. Interesting." Flossie sat in her nightclothes and a robe on a couch in the corner. She put the book she'd been reading down on the side table next to her and crossed her legs. Leaning forward, she stuck her elbow on her knee and then cupped her chin with her palm. "You certainly do get yourself caught up in all manner of things that require explanations."

"What are you doing here?" Cory looked around the room to see if anything had been touched or moved. This was a sanctuary, one where no one but she was allowed to come. It hadn't been cleaned since the last time Ezra had been in here and only she had touched the many pieces and parts that he'd left waiting on the table for his return, which had never happened.

"I didn't move anything, and I understand this is a place only you want to have access to, but I also know we need to talk, and you need to either explain what you are doing and let me help, or you need to stop. You are getting too far in and not thinking of your safety."

Cory scoffed but Flossie cut her off.

"Mrs. Havershall is dead. Is that correct?"

"Yes, but that has nothing to do with Ezra."

"And you're positive about that? Mrs. Havershall is dead by the same hand that you think killed your childhood friend and another prostitute, and now Lord Havershall asks a favor which entails you talking to

Revelson who just happened to be released from jail. You don't find that a little too coincidental?"

That stopped Cory in her tracks. She dropped her skirt, letting the hem brush the floor and ignoring the gasp from Flossie at the rip in the front.

"Why would you say that?"

"What happened to your dress!"

"You answer first. My dress is inconsequential. Why did you say they must all be related?" Although the more she let it run around in her head, the more she could see a bunch of connections that would make far more sense than if they had nothing to do with each other.

"Because Havershall does nothing for no one without it benefitting him. And if he went to the magistrate, as I heard he did, and asked for Revelson to be released to see if he could force information from you, then my educated guess would be that they must be related in some way or there's no way that would work." Flossie rocked back on the couch, no longer leaning forward looking for information, but settled in as if waiting for some big explanation that Cory just didn't have.

"But how would they relate?" Cory paced back and forth on the wide-planked floor, sure she was probably shuffling dust down into the room below but not caring. "If they knew each other, or if all the killers are the same, then what are they looking for? Or what are they trying to hide?" She turned one last time and faced Flossie head on. "And how do you know so much when you've been here all night?"

"Well, see my coach is faster than yours, and once I saw that you were in Reardon's company and no longer with Revelson I decided I did not need to wait to see the rest of the opera from down in the pit."

Cory could do nothing but stare at her cousin.

"Who do you think sent that lovely Mr. Reardon after you? Or supplied him with tickets to the box right next to yours?"

"You didn't!"

But Flossie looked far too pleased with herself for it to be untrue. "I did, and I'd do it again if I had to. You're in too deep, cousin of mine. You aren't thinking straight and you're putting yourself in harm's way far too many times for me to be comfortable. I did some divination right after you left and saw that things could potentially get out of hand. Yet I also saw that there would be a type of savior if I could get there in time. So, I did. You're welcome."

Cory was hard-pressed to thank her though. That could have gone horribly wrong. "Why did you take the chance of being seen? Havershall specifically said not to come to the opera. You could have jeopardized everything."

Scoffing, Flossie raised an eyebrow. "Use that brain of yours, Cory. This is dangerous. Too dangerous to play by anyone else's rules, and you know it. Besides, think of what Ezra would say if he could talk to you now."

"Fortunately, that can't happen since I very securely put his soul to rest." She hadn't meant to say that out loud since it was a secret only she was aware of, but now that it was in the air she couldn't take it back.

"Now it's my turn to ask that you didn't actually do that."

"I did. I have too many ghosts haunting me, and I didn't want Ezra to be able to come back and be another constant voice in my ear. As a murder victim you know there was every chance he would be looking for justice and unsure if he was even dead. He could have thought that he was simply dreaming of me and follow me around endlessly until he figured out he was actually dead and then things could have gotten worse. I wasn't willing to do that to him."

"Or yourself."

"Yes, okay? I wasn't willing to do that to myself either."

"We need to call him back." Flossie rose from the couch and headed for the corner where Cory kept her tools for scrying and for dealing with the dead.

Cory scampered across the room, determined to cut her off before she could get her hands on anything. "We can't."

"Of course we can. You can explain to him what happened and then put him back to sleep, but we have to know if he saw who killed him, or if there's anything he can do to help us. We're in danger, Cory, if you haven't noticed. Larkin was already here right after my divination. I didn't call him to come after you, I sent him after you. He told me you were in danger, and I got him next to you to save you if he had to, which he did. This is not a game. This isn't you and Ezra thinking your way through the universe and taking turns being eloquent for hours about how things are connected and how the world might be better if only they'd listen to the knowledge of the past. Waxing eloquent is going to get you killed."

"I haven't waxed anything, I'll have you know."

"Well, maybe you should..." Flossie said the words quietly, and Cory had no idea why she chuckled at the end of them. This was not funny.

Flossie regained her seriousness. "No more parlor tricks, Cory. The time is nigh and the moon is full, we must train our eyes on the information we can pull. Scry once for me and another time for yourself, bring forth your husband to answer and do so with stealth."

"Rhyming is not needed," Cory grumped.

"I know that, but things were getting too serious. Now look, I know that you feel a loyalty to that poor girl who died so horrendously and then was essentially put in a pauper's grave. I also know that originally we thought that had nothing to do with you. I did however understand wanting to find out what happened to her and make someone pay for it, as well as how that got you into trouble. You always were precocious. But this is more serious, and we need some backup or at least some more information. And there are only a few ways we can get it without sneaking into the police station and rifling through papers."

Tink, tink, thud. Tink, tink, thud. The sounds were familiar and would have been comforting had it not been impossible for her to hear them. Ezra's tools rattled on his workbench, disturbing the cobwebs and sending little plumes of dust into the air. The wobbly legs of the stool tucked beneath the worktable scuffed across the floor as it slid out from its hiding place.

Cory held her breath. Ezra was here.

CHAPTER 13

"Ezra." Cory's lungs seized and her heart constricted. He was here in the attic he'd converted into a workshop long before she'd taken up residence in Elmcroft Manor as his wife.

Even in death he took her breath away. Literally and figuratively. The afterlife had been kind to Ezra. So had the manner of his death. Poison worked from the inside out and unlike a knife or bullet often left no physical trace. At least externally. With newer, more radical medical and investigative practices in place, very few poisons remained untraceable.

All the more reason for her to keep certain species in her garden to herself.

"But how?" Coriander glanced at her cousin, accusation pinching the corners of her eyes as they narrowed in on their target. "What have you done, Flossie?"

Without unraveling the spell she cast on Ezra's grave or invoking one with the use of her scrying mirror, his apparition should not have been hovering anywhere within the walls of the home they once shared together.

"Don't look at me." Flossie raised her hands shoulder high in a placating gesture, before pushing to her feet and examining Ezra's spectral form. "I didn't conjure him."

"You must have. With that silly rhyme, no doubt." Cory gestured to her husband's spirit wafting about the rafters. "How else would you explain this?"

"Dear cousin, if rhyming words were all that were required to free a spirit from their coffin, the graves and cemeteries would empty every time a group of children sang Ring-a-Ring-a-Rosie." Flossie's head tilted to one side, her index finger tapping a slow rhythm against her lips. She circled around Ezra's translucent form the way the children did when they sang the little folk song she mentioned—with less skip in her step, of course. "It is peculiar though isn't it? Perhaps your need for justice is so great...well, there's nothing to be done about it now. He's here, ask the man himself."

Coriander feared this would happen and dreaded the moment it did. She took great pain in sealing her husband's grave so the only direction he could travel was toward his afterlife. She could have reversed the spell, and would have if her cousin had her way, but doing so would have left its mark on her soul. A high cost for a simple séance. Which was precisely why she'd crafted the spell that way—and never performed it.

Yet, there he was flitting about their attic in a hectic and hurried state as he often was in life when engrossed in the construction of one of his inventions.

"Ezra, darling?" Coriander's voice and footsteps were soft, almost timid.

Not at all the forceful tone she took with the young Mrs. Havershall. Of course, Ezra hadn't tried to possess her. At least, not yet. The horrid thought sent a shudder through her body. The things he might uncover in her mind if he were to take possession of her. And with that, another thought occurred to her. One that left guilt and remorse gnawing at her from the inside out. Had the spark of attraction between Mr. Reardon and herself been enough to rouse her husband from his grave? It was commonplace for a widow or widower to not only reenter society but to remarry. Not that she was interested in either—as she professed to her cousin on more than one occasion. While her interactions with the SPR investigator had been unconventional, they were in no way inappropriate.

Still, Ezra's presence gave her pause as he floated down from the rafters. Something had forced him from his resting place. What was it though?

"Darling, can you hear me?" She moved to intercept his spirit form, stopping him from flitting back and forth between the desk and workbench.

"Cory." Ezra's ghost turned his attention from the desk to her, warming her heart with one of his sheepish grins that emphasized the slight dimple in his cheek and brought out the glint in his eye. A look he often gave her when she found him a little disheveled and more than a little distracted tinkering with his inventions. "Have you seen my watch? I thought I left it on my desk. I've been searching everywhere."

Eza had been a man of singular focus once he started working on a new invention and often misplaced items about the house. For a moment she lost herself in the familiarity of her husband toiling in his workshop while she tended her garden and crafted a new potion for her personal stores.

"His watch?" Flossie's frustration snapped Cory out of her memories. Her cousin raised her hands and let them fall at her sides, pursing her lips. "What in Goddess's name could he possibly need with a watch? The dead don't keep time."

Flossie whispered the last, taking care not to shock Ezra with the truth of his condition. Without having been called and guided from the grave back to the earthly plane, a spirit may not realize they didn't reside among the living any longer. The news could be quite upsetting for all involved.

Yet another reason Cory didn't dabble in spiritualism.

"Your watch... Oh, Ezra. Your watch." Cory exclaimed, clasping her hands together as she beamed at her cousin. "His watch."

"Yes, we've established he wants his watch." Flossie blinked slowly as she worked through her frustration and confusion over the importance of a timepiece. "How does that help us?"

"Let's find out." Cory removed her reticule from around her wrist, opened the bag and retrieved the gold pocket watch.

"You found it. I've been searching high and low." Ezra reached for the watch in an effort to reclaim it, but his fingers slipped right through the gold, glass, and gears. He tried again, head cocked to one side, brows furrowed as he watched his fingers slide right through the timepiece.

Not a second later he disappeared, startling Coriander and Flossie both with his abrupt exit. Only to have them clutching their chests and gasping for breath when he popped back into existence near his workbench and began pacing again.

"What the devil?" Cory's gaze flicked between her husband's spirit sprinting from one side of his attic workspace to the other, kicking up a whirlwind of blueprints, cogs, and springs. "This is highly unusual."

"Not where you're involved, cousin. Unusual is anything but, where you're concerned." Flossie gave a frantic wave of her hand, encouraging her cousin to do something, anything to stop the building energy in the small space. "Well?"

"Well, what? It was your idea to raise Ezra. Why don't you think of a way to put him back to rights?" Cory snatched papers from the air and set them back on his desk, followed by the springs and gears; repeated the process when he knocked them over again.

"Cory." Ezra turned to look at her again. "My watch. Have you seen it?"

The words weren't precisely the same, but the message was clear. Ezra wanted the watch—or for Coriander to have the watch. Now, she just had to parcel out why.

"Here it is. You left it on your desk." She played along and held out the watch for Ezra, hoping she did the right thing or said the right word to trigger a new response from his ghost.

But the pattern continued.

"You found it. I've been searching everywhere."

Not for the first time, and certainly not the last, Coriander wondered why the Goddess set her on this path following a string of dead bodies in search of the clues required to uncover their murderer.

A murderer who may have very well started his killing spree with her husband.

Was that why? Perhaps it was Ezra, and not Franny after all, that connected her to all of this. She gave it a moment's contemplation. The thought swirled in her mind like brandy in a snifter and considered it much the same way one would the layers of a glass of liquor—she used her senses. But instead of the mortal sense of sight, taste, and smell, she reached for something more.

Something magical.

Coriander opened her third eye and examined Ezra's limited apparition. His ghost was but a trace, a fraction when compared to the young Lady Havershall's. No doubt a residual piece of his soul that seeped out before her binding spell prior to his funeral. Something that shouldn't have happened and wouldn't have happened if she'd bound anyone other than her husband. Or possibly Flossie or Esther. Emotions wreaked havoc with intentions, and grief was a powerful emotion.

Yes, she decided. It must have been her emotions tangled up in the spell that left a part of Ezra behind.

There was simply no other explanation for it. Ezra wasn't a witch. He couldn't have manipulated spirits or anything else for that matter. His inventions rarely worked properly without her magical intervention and even then, they never seemed to function quite as they were supposed to. No, he couldn't possibly have found a way to transfer a sliver of his spiritual essence into a pocket watch.

"Preposterous," she muttered to herself, resting her hands on her hips, as she pulled on the memory niggling at the back of her mind... "Or was it? Egypt is a wondrous place with old magic."

She paced the floor, ignoring Ezra's spirit and the clatter of his tools for a moment, and talking to herself about temples, tombs, and powerful spells to transcend this life and the next.

"Cory?" Flossie gripped the ends of the velvet belt around her robe and cinched it tight around her waist. "What in Goddess name are you prattling on about? What do pyramids and pharaohs have to do with any of this?"

"Nothing? Everything?" Coriander had no idea what it all meant. At least not yet. She was still working on the connection, but she was certain of at least one thing.

For the first time since Ezra died, she felt she was on the right track.

She thought she had been with Timothy, but this kindling, this spark of connection between Ezra's essence, Egypt, and the dead women there in London was different than what she felt when she urged the inspector to pursue her husband's business partner. She might have felt guilty over that realization had he not done the same to her—*first* she might add, and not because he believed she was the killer, but because she made a convenient scapegoat. No, try as she might,

Coriander couldn't muster so much as a pang of remorse where Timothy Revelson was concerned.

"Yes, all right. I can see you're still working that part out, but what about the watch? And Ezra?" Flossie lowered her voice to a whisper that only Cory could hear when she spoke his name and jerked her head in his direction.

"Well, that's just it, isn't it, cousin?" Coriander rested her hands on her hips, the disarray of her appearance after the events at the theater long forgotten and focused on the spot where the ghost of her husband sat.

She hesitated, reconsidering whether she should share her hypothesis with Flossie. Not from fear that her cousin would cast off the idea, failing to believe her. No, quite the opposite. It was Coriander who was afraid. Afraid that Flossie *would believe her*—that she was right. And if she was, the implications that followed. She closed her eyes, pulled in a deep cleansing breath, steadied her nerves enough to forge ahead, and shared her theory with Flossie.

"Ezra shouldn't be here. I bound him after the funeral and neither of us reversed that spell to call him here tonight." Coriander turned the pocket watch over and over in her hand, admiring the intricate details as if seeing them for the first time. "This isn't his ghost."

"Not his ghost? The ethereal form of your very dead husband is sitting at his workbench. If that is not an apparition, I would very much like to hear what *you think it is*." Flossie eyed Coriander with wary apprehension as if expecting her to deliver more bad news.

Coriander didn't begrudge the look in her cousin's eyes. With so much talk of dead women, the arrival of an SPR investigator who seemed to know more than he should, and the senior Lord Havershall who definitely knew more than he should, Flossie had every right to be wary.

Because Coriander was as well.

"A part of Ezra's essence." She wrung her hands and shook her head, struggling to share the next part. What she feared would be the worst part. "Perhaps, even a part of his soul."

"What?" Flossie's exclamation was enough to startle Ezra's apparition, resetting him at the beginning of his loop with inquiries about the blasted pocket watch. She waited for Coriander to produce the watch and finish the routine before rounding on her cousin. "Explain yourself, Cory. What do you mean a part of his soul? He wouldn't survive it. How could such a thing be possible?"

"The same way that magic is possible, cousin." Coriander raised her hand, halting the argument poised on Flossie's lips before she could launch herself into a tirade. "Dear, sweet Ezra was no different than any other mortal. Not an ounce of magical energy within his body. But he had a soul, pure and perfect, and that's a bit of magic in its own right, isn't it? That spark inside us, that makes us who we are, animates our thoughts and feelings. Each one unique and yet, a commonality that makes us all the same. The fact that it exists at all is magical."

"While I'd argue the purity of the vast majority of souls in London, I can follow that logic. Souls are their own form of magic. Perhaps what separates a witch from a regular human is the ability to harness that magic and wield it for our own purpose." Flossie moved in front of Coriander, who had begun pacing the floor again, and stopped her in her tracks. She clasped her cousin's hands between hers and gave a reassuring squeeze. "I'm not sure I'm following the rest, Cory, but I am listening and I will believe you. Trust in that. Now, explain to me why making a connection to souls and magic is important and what it has to do with Ezra's watch and the murders here in London?"

Coriander felt a twang of unease beneath her breastbone, the bubbles of nerves in the back of her throat, but she pressed on. Her cousin spoke the truth. If anyone would believe her it would be Flossie.

And Larkin.

She had the distinct feeling that the inspector for the Society of Paraphysical Research trusted her and would believe whatever she had to say about the subject at hand. Her unease was replaced with a spark of interest, and perhaps something more, but she pushed all of that aside and forged ahead with her theory—as frightening as it was.

"Because, dear cousin, I believe Ezra discovered a way to bottle magic."

Coriander held out the pocket watch and pressed the button, popping open the cover to expose the watch face. She glanced over at Ezra's ethereal form back at his work bench, relishing the memory of the conversations they'd shared in this room, and then she snapped the watch shut. And he disappeared from her life once more. She rubbed a fist over her heart, grateful the pain of losing him a second time was far less than it had been the first.

"Bottle magic?" Flossie went white as a sheet, her sickly pallor not far from that of Ezra's apparition. "You can't be serious? But of course, you are. I know I said I would believe you, and I do, Coriander, I do. This is just... Bottle magic...Are you certain?"

Flossie had taken to pacing and Coriander couldn't help but join her at her side. They lapped the attic workspace in tense silence until Flossie asked, "But why the pocket watch? What's the significance? Why would he put a piece of his soul there and not your wedding band?"

"For the same reason I brought it to the opera this evening." Coriander produced the pocket watch again, this time turning the crown to wind the gears. "It's a recording device."

Coriander just hoped she hadn't destroyed whatever message Ezra had left her. If he'd gone to the trouble of tampering with his soul, she knew it was of the utmost importance—and that it would not be good news.

CHAPTER 14

Cory opened the pocket watch again, this time expecting Ezra to come back into the attic and not surprised when he did. Because she was ready, she was able to take more in about his form. The way he seemed to shift in and out of focus. He was in a loop that would probably continue until she found out what he needed her to know.

And she was bound and determined to get that answer as soon as possible. Before he started talking, she jumped right in. "Here, Ezra. Here's your watch. What is it about the watch that you need to tell me?"

"You found my watch, thank you, my dear."

He still couldn't touch it, but he did try to pass his hand through yet again. While it was a pleasure to be able to see Ezra again it was also painful to stand by while he couldn't do anything. It made her resolve even stronger to find out what the watch signified so that

Ezra could rest in peace and not have to endlessly and fruitlessly ask for his timepiece from here to eternity.

But what could she do? She glanced over at Flossie, but she just shrugged her shoulders.

"You don't have any ideas?" Cory whispered. "I need to do something or this is not going to stop. I can't let him loop forever, Flossie. It will destroy me to know he is up here over and over again trying to get his hands on his watch."

"I'm sorry, Cory. I don't know what to tell you, I don't have any experience with this. My word, this is horrendous." Her eyes darted back and forth as Ezra moved through the room with purpose.

He needed to do something to be released, but Cory didn't know what. She pawed through the papers on his desk, looking for anything that would clue her in to why he'd done this. Had he made notes about what he was here for?

Desperation clawed up her throat and tears leaked from her eyes. Why this form? Why did he compromise his spirit when he had to know this was a terrible idea?

She sat down in his chair and leaned forward with her elbows on her knees and her forehead in her upturned hands. "There's too much death and too many unanswered questions. I didn't sign up for this. I just wanted to know what happened to my old friend. I didn't want her death to go unnoticed by those who should have taken better care of her. She died for nothing, and now I have a spirit who will wander for all the years to come trying to get a damn watch when what I need is my husband here!" At the end she was screaming and honestly, she did not give a bloody care. Let someone come and take her to an insane asylum. Let someone think she was unfit to live on her own and give the house to Ezra's brother.

She was tired and she was done.

The sobs didn't take her off guard as much as they felt like they cleansed her of all the dirt and smudge that she had been holding in, trying to figure out life after the rug had been yanked out from under her feet.

She was a strong woman, she knew that. She had been left alone on her own for months on end and had always managed to make sure she tended to the house and had the bills paid. No debt collector had ever had to come and tell her that he could no longer extend her credit due to non-payment.

There had always been food in the pantry and when she knew Ezra was on his way home, she would lay in supplies to make all the foods he loved and missed while he was in Egypt. There were dishes that they just did not have the food on hand there to make him. But she did. She and Esther would spend days beforehand making his favorite pies, preparing meat and cheese and vegetables in the ways that he would have missed.

Through her tears, she smiled for the first time in a long time while remembering Ezra.

And when he finally arrived, she would run out to the drive the second she heard the carriage turn onto the gravel and she'd be waiting for him on the front steps. Well, to be honest, she usually ran down the drive and he'd have the coachman halt the conveyance so that she could jump in without the step and sit nestled against Ezra's side while she held his hand.

And he'd show her the pocket watch and tell her how important it was. How it held all his dreams and all the things he'd learned in his travels. She never quite understood what exactly he meant, but she was always so happy to be back in his presence that she would just nod along with whatever he was saying, overjoyed to bask in having him back on the estate.

She felt a hand on her head. It stroked her hair. Flossie had to see how much she was hurting and just wanted to comfort her but the gesture was so Ezra, one he made every time he was going to leave her again to go travel the world, a world she didn't want because everything she needed was here, except her husband. Until he came back. But even that was no longer true.

"Um, don't panic, Cory, but Ezra has broken out of his loop, and um, he appears to be trying to comfort you. I think."

Cory very slowly and carefully lifted her head. And Ezra's hand slid down the side of her face then cupped her chin as it had all those times he'd say goodbye.

"I am having so much trouble living without you," Cory whispered. "Why did you have to go?"

"My love, there are things in this world that we will never understand. I have but one moment with you and I'm sorry that it has made you cry. If I could I would come back to you, but this was the best I could do. He's coming for you. I need you to protect yourself and you can only do that with the wa—"

His shade snapped out of the room, one moment here and the next gone. Cory felt the lack in her bones and knew that no matter what she did he would not be coming back. At least he was at rest now.

"We need to figure out the watch. Is there anyone within the community that you know that Ezra might have talked to? Anyone he had dealings with that I wouldn't know about?" Flossie was far more involved with business dealings than Cory had ever been. Cory had often faded back into the manor, leaving daily life to other people, and not wanting to do anything more than tend her flowers and quietly exist so as not to draw attention to herself. But Flossie was too inquisitive and too involved to have lived in the same way.

"I don't know much about what he did," Flossie said, "but my husband was surprised that Ezra was having dealings with a few of the ton who had less nobility on their mind and more need for funds. Times are changing, and it is no longer enough to come from money especially with the nouveau riche coming up through the ranks as shipping magnates and leaders of industry. Ezra always seemed to have new ideas and a way of executing them as effortlessly as possible. Many were seeking him out to see if any of his inventions might be used to bring in coin."

"His inventions? Why would they think those could be sold for anything?"

Flossie shrugged. "Because you infused them with magic and made them work, but no one knew that. He often talked about them as if they were the next wonder of the world. A way to make a maid's job easier and free her up to do other tasks. People thought fewer servants and more work would save them money."

"I mean that could be true, but every design had flaws."

"Flaws that you fixed for the ones he shared with people."

"He did?"

"Oh yes, he often brought that cleaning thing over and entertained people with the way it could sweep a floor within minutes and leave it was cleaner than any one person could do in twice the time. He had backers just ready to produce them in factories if he'd give them the designs."

"He never told me that." Cory tracked back through their many conversations and paused because that was not necessarily true. He had told her a number of times that he looked forward to the day when he might be able to make the machines affordable for people so that they could spend more time doing things that brought them joy. She had nodded and then shown him her newest plants and talked about how she might need to till some more land in the backyard to plant more seeds. He'd smile and then tell her that perhaps he could make something that would dig up the ground for her so that she could spend more time sewing or reading. With him.

She would not cry again. She would not lament that she'd missed so many opportunities to step outside herself and her desires to see what he had wanted to do.

But she would instead concentrate on the fact that her magic was the one thing that often made his inventions work and perhaps using her magic on the watch would be just the answer this time. She was listening anyway, and that might be all that was needed.

"Is the watch back on the desk?" she asked Flossie, standing from the chair and fluffing out the skirt of her dress.

Flossie nodded and pointed to where the timepiece teetered on the edge of the massive desk Ezra had inherited from his father.

"Okay, let's see what he has to say."

"Are you sure you want to touch it again? What if he comes back?"

"I'm certain he won't this time, Flossie. He said what he wanted me to hear, and it's up to us to figure this out from here. Now, do you see the pouch and the box he kept the watch in?"

The timepiece would hang from a chain when Ezra wore it but every night, he would put it away as if protecting it. And maybe he had been. She had thought it was cute and unnecessary, but she had thought that about many things and was coming to find out that perhaps she'd been wrong and had not given him enough credit.

Flossie brought the box and the pouch to the desk, and Cory centered the three pieces on the blotter that Ezra had made many notes on over the years. It had diagrams and pictures, ideas, and upgrades galore. She didn't understand them all, but with the three in a triangle she saw what she had thought she'd remembered when she'd come in to see if he had forgotten about dinner.

With a slight shift of all three obkects, she lined them up with a square and two circles on the blotter. Her mind clicked on an image from years ago and she switched the watch with the pouch, making sure that the mouth of the pouch was open and facing down.

There was a glow for just an instant, a blue nimbus that Cory had seen before but had always thought was a candle or a burner that Ezra would snuff out as soon as she entered the room. Often, she'd been afraid of him using fire this high up in the house and with no water nearby in case the flame jumped in the breeze that usually came through the open window behind him.

She placed her hands on the table as she'd seen him do before, bowed her head, and forced energy into the bracket her hands made around the three objects.

The glow grew and grew. The pouch's strings danced on the blotter, the box lid opened and closed, and then the watch lid flipped open. The hands on the clock face spun faster and faster, until Cory was afraid she might be nauseous from dizziness.

And then a voice filled the room.

"Yes, if only we could bottle it, I guarantee we could make a fortune. You and me, Ezra. We could revolutionize the world with this new discovery, and you would be the greatest inventor anyone had ever seen. Better than even the greatest mage in all of Egypt. Forget about tomes of legends from scribes from thousands of years ago. This would be a discovery like never before!"

Cory glanced at Flossie, who shrugged. Neither of them recognized the voice.

"I'm not sure. I'd like to think that it could help people. I'm not looking for revolution. I just want to help people." Ezra sounded skeptical, and Cory felt the same.

"But, Ezra, this could be everything. And if Coriander would help us, we'd be able to make sure it could reach the entire world in months. Just mere months!"

"Let me..."

The voice trailed off and then a new voice entered the room.

"Find the financier, clear my name, and I will take that secret to my grave, Coriander. You have my word."

"Wait," Flossie said, leaning in. "Who's that and what was Ezra saying?"

Cory's stomach rolled. "That's Timothy from the opera box when I had the watch with me. I must have captured his voice and cut off what Ezra had been trying to tell me."

What were they going to do now?

CHAPTER 15

"He knows." Cory felt the blood recede from her upper extremities to pool in her feet, chasing after her heart and stomach that felt as though they'd dropped into an abyss.

"Who? What do they know?" Flossie was a lot of things, but she wasn't a dolt. She may not have known the answer to the former, but Cory suspected she came to the same conclusion about the latter as she had.

Timothy Revelson spoke the truth.

Her secret was well and truly out. The public persona she had crafted with such painstaking care was nothing more than fodder for the ton's gossip and the socialite columns in the papers. The sacrifices made and freedoms gained when she married Ezra and took the Whitlock name obliterated as if by cannon fire. A drop and a sudden stop were all that awaited her. Her hands were at her neck, fingertips pressed against her throat as if the hangman's noose were already tightened around it.

"The financier. He's the voice on Ezra's recording." Cory was certain of it. Another piece of the puzzle snapped into place. But another problem presented itself. She knew the role, quite possibly the purpose, but had no name. The next piece of the puzzle was missing.

"That's all well and good, cousin, but we still don't know who *he is*." Flossie stressed, mirroring her own thoughts.

"No, we do not." Coriander's brows pinched together, and she tapped her index finger against her lips in a nervous rhythm. "This financier, whoever he is, has put a lot of time, and I suspect money into, in keeping his identity a secret. Otherwise, Ezra would still be alive."

"Yes, and all the more reason for us to stop this madness now." Flossie marched toward the attic door and swung it open, gesturing to the stairway with a sweep of her arm. "We need to leave the city. We'll go to my country estate."

"We need help," Cory admitted at the same time her cousin suggested they retreat. She blinked once, twice, unable to hide the shock from her face and voice. "You want me to run? To hide?"

"You always favored Sardines, Cory, even though you only played once." The old wooden floor planks creaked beneath Flossie's feet as she hurried away from the door and back to Cory's side, grasping her hands. "If the voice Ezra captured on his recording device is to be believed, they found more than mummified kings in those tombs. They found a way to bottle magic. Or at least they think they have. Goddess...Franny. Did they kill her to take her magic?"

So, her cousin came to the same conclusion she had about the death of her childhood friend. If not the same way to handle it.

"They killed Ezra." Coriander raised her hand, staving off Flossie's protests that that was all the more reason for them to abandon Elmcroft and what remained of the life she had built here. "They know who and what I am, Flossie. Where I go will be of no consequence. The countryside, the seaside, America. It doesn't matter. They will find me eventually."

Flossie mashed her lips into a thin line, pressed her hands against her hips, and glared at her. The worn area rug softened the thump of her slippered foot as she tapped an angry beat against the floor. "And I suppose you have a better idea? One utterly lacking when it comes to self-preservation, no doubt. Go on, then. Out with it."

"Pursuing the financier is dangerous, you're right about that." Cory ignored the arched brow and haughty expression on her cousin's face and powered on. "We need help, and I know just the man for the job."

"You can't possibly think the Special Inspector is... Oh, no, Coriander Whitlock. Absolutely not." Flossie's hands moved from her waist and were tucked firm against her ribcage as she crossed her arms over her chest and squared her shoulders. "I forbid it."

"You forbid it? That, dear cousin, is the epitome of hypocrisy. It was you who enlisted his help and sent him to the opera earlier this evening, was it not?" Cory's gaze narrowed and matched Flossie's pose as she held her ground.

"I had a vision." Flossie's cheeks reddened with her rising voice and temper. "You fell Coriander. You would have died. I had to do something, and Mr. Reardon fit the bill of the man who prevented that from happening. *If* I chose to intervene. Which, of course, *I did*."

Cory's mind wandered a moment to the strength in Larkin's grip when he tugged her back from the railing in the private box, the way her heart raced not just from her brush with death, but the look in his eyes. Until a fresh wave of betrayal and guilt pushed those thoughts away.

"I appreciate what you did, Flossie, but your reasons don't matter now. He had his suspicions before, but those have no doubt been solidified after his involvement at the opera house tonight."

Cory softened her posture, her shoulders relaxed and hands clasped in front of her as she tried to convince her cousin that Larkin Reardon was their best hope of stopping Ezra's killer from reaching his goal—and their best chance at survival.

"Besides, he has skills. Skills he no doubt honed over the years working for the investigative branch of one of England's most secret societies. If anyone has the resources to help us uncover the financier's name, it's Mr. Reardon."

Flossie closed her eyes and let out a long, slow exhale as she pinched the bridge of her nose. "I can't believe I am going to say this, but you're right. Send word for Mr. Reardon. Invite him to join us for tea tomorrow."

Cory flicked her gaze to the small porthole window at the far end of the attic and the first signs of the night's retreat in the lightening sky on the other side of the glass and corrected her cousin. "Invite him for tea today."

In the end, Flossie had agreed, even supported her idea to enlist the aid of Mr. Reardon. She also demanded they retire to their rooms and get some rest in anticipation of his arrival later that day. She woke Henry, her coachman, before she retired and gave him instructions to deliver the invitation to Larkin personally at the earliest reasonable hour.

Wound tighter than Ezra's watch, sleep eluded Coriander. The first tendrils of light slithered through the sky, peeling back the layer of inky blackness and shades of gray. A hint of pastels softened the view outside her bedroom. She threw the covers back, slid from her bed and into her slippers, wrapped her robe around her, cinching it about her waist, and went to the kitchen for her first of several pots of tea.

By the time Larkin Reardon was set to arrive, Coriander's nerves set all the tea she consumed sloshing about in her stomach. She glanced at the table where the silver tray laden with little cakes and sandwiches, of sweet and savory varieties, sat beside her best porcelain service, complete with a pot of her bergamot blend steeped to perfection. The thought of another cup rolled her stomach like a ship caught in a rogue wave in the Atlantic.

"For goddess's sake, Cory, sit down." Flossie tucked away the needlepoint design she'd begun to occupy her time before Mr. Reardon arrived and turned her focus to her cousin. "It's not as if the man is here to propose. Though it's high time someone did."

She muttered the last under her breath, though Coriander heard every word. Where irritation would have bloomed within her and set a frown upon her face over such a statement when her cousin first arrived, Cory couldn't help the smile that settled on her face from the normalcy of her words. Death came calling once more and the original purpose of Flossie's trip had been forgotten. While she had no intention of remarrying, she much preferred the idea of evading the clutches of a prospective husband then a hangman.

"Madam, Mr. Reardon." With a soft knock and a formal introduction, Henry drew her back from the thoughts darkening her mind and her mood.

"Mrs. Thompson, Ms. Whitlock." Larkin Reardon stepped out from behind Henry, his hat tucked under one arm and a small package wrapped in decorative paper under the other, and gave a curt bow. "I can't say as I am disappointed to find myself in your company this afternoon, though I was surprised to have received an invitation so soon after our last encounter."

He greeted them both as he crossed the room, his gaze traveling from Flossie seated in a gold velvet Damask tufted armchair she had claimed for herself before settling on Coriander, who had stopped midstride to the left of the fireplace.

Coriander noted that his eyes did not meet hers. In fact, with a slight tilt of his head and dip of his chin, he seemed fixated on a different part of her anatomy located lower on her body. Past the buttons fastened down the center of her blouse, to her waist where the hem was neatly tucked beneath the cinch of her skirt. The same place where his hands had been the night before when he'd saved her life. Heat flushed her skin—especially above her hips where she still felt his hands, as if he'd branded the shape of them into her flesh.

A reaction she blamed on her frazzled state and proximity to the heat billowing out of the fireplace.

"I believe we're beyond such formalities, Larkin." When had Coriander become so bold? She noted her cousin's widened eyes and assumed she must have wondered the same thing, before she flicked the thought away and returned her focus back to the man and the task before her.

"Coriander, it's a pleasure to see you again." Larkin's full lips curved at the corner in a devilish smile. Her name rolled off his tongue in the smooth, deep timber of his voice. It sounded different than when Ezra said it. Different, but she realized she liked the sound of it nonetheless.

"Likewise." She fought not to match his smile with one of her own. What was it about this man who frustrated and all but threatened to reveal her to the SPR? Whatever it was, it was irrelevant to the reason she and Flossie had invited him to Elmcroft. Best she kept her mind on the problems at hand rather than welcome another. "Flossie and I have found ourselves in a bit of a predicament and in need of your assist... Oh, is that for us? How rude of me, do accept my apologies."

Coriander looked to the parcel Larkin had moved from under the crook of his arm and held in his hand.

"How thoughtful." She crossed the room, the tips of her boots peeking out from the hem of her skirt as she moved and took the package from him. She made short work of the ribbon, letting it fall away, and peeled back the lid of the white paper box. "What...what is this?"

"I wish I could take credit, but the gift was on your doorstep. I'm merely the deliveryman."

Cory stood like a stone statue, only glancing up to find Larkin's eyes narrowed, his brows furrowing. Had he noticed the wabble in her usual confident tone and in the slight tremor in her otherwise steady hands as she rifled through the tufts of tissue paper within the box. Even when he appeared outside her house in the middle of the night, all but accusing her of practicing the craft, she hadn't been this ruffled. She didn't like it, and from his expression neither did he.

"Let me see, Coriander. Show it to me." His voice barely managed not to bark the command, and she could see the way he forced himself to resist the urge to snatch the box from her. She too was resisting smashing what was inside that had her so upset into a million pieces. Larkin waited for her to reveal it to him with his fists curled at his sides.

"It's..." Eyes wide, Coriander shook her head, a mix of shock and horror swirling in the depths of her mind. "It's a funeral biscuit." She flicked her gaze to Flossie, lips pursed as she regained control over the emotions that fought to rule her. Cory straightened her spine, steeled her voice, and met Larkin's worried gaze. "With my initials on it."

CHAPTER 16

She of course was not the only person to have ever sported the initials C.W. And if she had found the biscuit in a bakery, she might have been able to admire it and wish whoever planned her funeral would order them someday in the distant future when it was her time to go to the great beyond.

Perhaps she could have even considered it a gift from someone who was not aware that this wasn't just a decorated biscuit alone.

But the note in the box, the one addressed to her full name so there was no mistaking it was for her, very quickly disabused her of any other notion than that it was a threat.

"Dearest Coriander, I hope this finds you well and truly happy. I am certain that with the unexpected death of your friend, Timothy, you will want to attend his funeral in full support of such a friend to your late and great husband. I will be there also, watching you to make sure that you do not do anything untoward. May this serve as notice to you that Timothy was not the only one with information that you might want to keep hidden. It would only take one word for your entire world to change, and I'm prepared to speak that one word. May your day be bright and your blessings...plentiful..."

It was only ended with one word that made no sense. No signature. It made Cory's stomach feel like it was rising into her throat and choking her. No signature and no way to know from whom it came. Unless...

"Flossie, can you please go speak with all the staff and see if anyone witnessed a package being dropped off this morning? Even if it was a courier, perhaps that would get us some answers about who we are dealing with."

Flossie sputtered, but Cory shot her a look that brooked no argument.

"For me, Flossie, please. I'm sure Mr. Reardon will keep his hands to himself and his conversation polite. I need you to do this."

Flossie harrumphed but did indeed leave with one last narrow-eyed glance that she spotlighted both Cory and Larkin with before leaving the room but not closing the door.

"She is not happy," Cory's guest observed and if the situation wasn't so dire, Cory might have laughed. As it was, there was a part of her that wanted to go back to that flutter she'd experienced in the opera house box last night just to feel anything but despair for the first time in a very long time.

But she mustn't. She had important things to do, and Larkin had been invited here to help her do them.

Now that she'd received this letter and biscuit, it was even more necessary to secure Larkin's help. Hopefully before anyone else had to die.

Placing the cookie back into the ornate box, Cory tapped the letter on the point of her chin. "How likely are you to help us without knowing the full story?"

He shot his cuffs and sat in the chair opposite her, taking his time in smoothing the line of his trousers and making sure his shirt was tucked neatly into the waistband. Right before Cory wanted to ask the question again in case he hadn't heard her, he whipped his head up and gazed directly into her eyes. It was unnerving, but she did very much appreciate the direct approach instead of beating around the bush.

"I would call it highly unlikely if you want the nice answer and absolutely not going to happen if you'd like it a little more basic."

"Fair enough. I will neither confirm nor deny what or who I am. I will leave it at that someone is pulling strings and has an end goal that I cannot allow to happen. In the pursuit of this goal, this person is bringing down anyone and anything near to him that would perhaps stand in his way." Larkin opened his mouth and she held up a hand. "I do not know who he is, and I do not know exactly what the end game is, but it has caused several deaths of good people and some not-so-good people. It must stop."

"And tell me then why you don't have your Special Inspector here? Surely, he'd be willing and able, probably even champing at the bit like an eager horse if given the chance to solve all these murders and put a horrible man behind bars at the Old Bailey. So why me?"

He leaned forward in his chair, and Cory's breath backed up in her lungs due to their closeness. She could see the specks of gold in his eyes, and they mesmerized her.

"Why me, Coriander Whitlock? Why me?"

"I..." She trailed off because so many thoughts were going through her mind and she couldn't grab hold of any one of them. She looked down at her hands, at the letter gripped tight in her fist, and steeled herself against everything that her life had become since her husband's death. "Because you are the only one I will trust to help me right this wrong, all of these wrongs. I don't want the police. I don't want to do this the nice way, or the correct way. I don't want to have to sit through and testify at another court case as I watch my world die around me." She huffed out a breath. "I am not asking you to do anything that would be entirely illegal, but I am tired of playing by the rules, Larkin. I am tired of doing everything I'm supposed to do and in the way the ton and society as a whole expects and still getting knocked to the floor over and over again. My husband was a good man and he did not deserve to die. If I can find the man who killed him with your help, then I will and can take care of the rest."

Her cheeks heated as he continued to stare at her from the short distance between them. Emotions ran across his face and through his eyes. She wished her talent had been reading minds instead of being able to make plants grow and thrive no matter the environment. It would be so much easier if she could know, really know, what he was thinking.

She'd spent her whole life doing what she was supposed to in order to fit into a society that would hate her and perhaps even execute her if they knew what she was. And yet really what she was only meant that she understood nature better than most, took care of the Mother Earth who allowed them to tread on her, and kept her nose in a botanical book. But even that was threatened, and all because some arsehole, and yes, she'd thought that word, wanted her essence in order to make money.

Ezra would never have gone with that, she knew it in her heart even if she'd accidentally recorded over the end of the conversation with the financier. But she needed help to track down this person and put a stop to him.

And if she had to trade her secrecy and her shadow self to be able to have justice for the man who'd loved her and the friends who did not deserve to die at this horrible monster's hands, then by damn, she was going to do whatever it took.

"I can almost see the smoke coming out of your ears." Larkin leaned back in his chair finally as if he'd come to a decision and was done weighing the odds and the request. "I'm intrigued by all of this, and because I've devoted my life to the cause and to the debunking of those who would swindle the innocent in the name of hocus-pocus. I also believe that what you are saying is truth. I've looked into more of the situation after last night's...shall we call it, an interlude? And there is far more going on than I was led to believe."

Despite the fact that Cory wanted to shout at him to just tell her if he would help her, she held her tongue.

Forcing him to do anything at this point was out of the question. He too could ruin her entire existence with only a few words as the letter writer had threatened, so she had no bargaining chips, only a plea for assistance and a hope that his conscience wouldn't allow him to say no.

"I will need to see the letter and any other pieces of this puzzle that you possess." He leaned forward again with one hand braced on his knee. "I know for a fact that you will not want to give me everything you have, and I expect that you will hold some information back simply because you might trust me but not with everything. I am willing to take that under advisement, but the more facts and clues you are willing to share, the closer we will be able to get to revealing this heinous person and making it so that even if there is a trial you would not be the one having to answer for any sins society thinks you might have committed."

Cory's heart fluttered in her chest the same as it did last night at the opera. His intense stare, the breadth of his shoulders, the fierceness in his gaze, all combined to make her body tingle in ways that she'd be afraid she was having a dizzy spell if she didn't know better.

He reached his other hand out to her. Was he wanting to shake on the deal? Did he want to hold her hand? She shook her head at herself briefly. He wanted the letter. Of course that was what he wanted. But when he took it from her outstretched hand, he lingered with his fingertips on the pulse at her wrist. A pulse that jumped and then sped along like a steam train careening down an abandoned track.

Mercy!

"Tell me everything," he said.

Cory started with the death of her husband and moved into the death of her friend, the séance that they both were at. She was deliberately vague about how the ghost of the dead wife had possessed her and what she'd had to do to get rid of her. But she did tell him about why she had been at the brothel and how she most certainly had not killed the woman in the room where she and Larkin had met.

"I tried to show the Special Inspector the picture of the ring I'd drawn off Kitty's description, but he did not take me seriously."

Larkin's stare was unnerving. His lowered brow made her afraid she'd not been clear in what she was saying or had only served in exposing herself but not highlighting the seriousness of the current situation.

"I'll need to hear the recording and see the picture of the ring."

She could have left him in the parlor and gone to get the items, but she was afraid to leave him alone just yet until she had his solid commitment that he would help and not hinder or ruin her chances at finding her husband's killer. She wasn't going to ask him to follow her to Ezra's private office because there were too many things in there that she couldn't explain.

Instead, she pulled the bell next to her chair and waited for one of Flossie's servants to arrive. They were almost a platoon so someone should be available to answer her call even as Flossie was interrogating them to see if anyone had heard or seen anything regarding the package delivery.

A slight woman Cory couldn't place showed up in a few moments.

"Ma'am?"

"Can you please get Esther for me?"

"Of course, ma'am." She curtsied and left.

"How many servants do you have?" Larkin asked into the silence.

"One. Everyone else is Flossie's." Cory fidgeted with the box in her lap.

"You run this entire estate with just you and one servant?"

"It is possible," Cory stated and set the box on the table next to her. "I've made decisions that I had to, and I will always survive."

"I don't doubt that at all. I just wonder if Ezra would be pleased to know he left you in such a state of despair and if he considered that if you did not have the resources to care for yourself that you would be forced to shutter much of the home he left to you."

Cory's whole body bristled up in indignation. Ezra had not intended to leave her at all. They'd never talked much about what would happen and what the finances were before he'd died because she had always expected him to come home.

Fortunately, she was saved from having to respond to Larkin by Esther's arrival.

"Ms. Coriander, you called?"

That was really quite formal for Esther, but Cory let it pass because she was not in the mood to chide her most treasured friend besides Flossie.

"Yes, Esther, if you could please retrieve my reticule..." Cory trailed off when Esther handed it over before she'd said the last word. "Thank you, Esther."

"Of course, ma'am. Will there be anything else?"

"No, I think we're okay." And Cory was not going to mention that the reason Esther would have known what she wanted and where to find it was most assuredly because Esther had been eavesdropping on her conversations with Flossie and Larkin. She'd thank her later.

Digging through the small purse, Cory found the folded paper she'd been carrying with her constantly, wanting to make sure she had it if she randomly caught sight of the ring and would need to use the picture to compare. She unfolded the small square and then handed it over to Larkin, making sure to pull back before he could touch her wrist again.

There was a quirk of his lips as Larkin took the paper and stared at it. He turned it left and right and upside down. "It's not very detailed," he said.

"I was drawing from someone's verbal cues. I did not see it but was told that the man who used to visit Franny had this ring on his finger. It has an emerald embedded in it."

"Interesting. The emerald could be the key to finding more information." He kept turning the paper around and around, tilting it to the window to get the best light. "I believe I have seen this ring before."

Cory gasped. It couldn't be that easy. But oh, how she would love for it to be that easy.

"The book is back at my lodgings."

Of course it wasn't going to be that easy.

"Do you have someone who could bring it to you here?"

He sighed. "There are a number of reasons that the answer to that is no. But the main one is that I would prefer to handle all of this by myself. The fewer hands we have in, the better we can keep certain information from getting to anyone else."

It made sense, but now what were they supposed to do?

"Shall we take one of Flossie's carriages and retrieve the book? I am sure I can have it ready in just a few moments." Especially since Esther was still hovering in the hallway right outside the door and most likely Henry, who she'd seen pass by a few minutes ago.

"I have my horse and that would be a lot faster. I could trot right on over and be back in no more time than it would take to prepare a carriage."

Cory's heart sank. If he left, he might never come back. If he walked out that door, he could have people swarming her property to fit her for a noose within an hour.

Larkin stood and drew her to her feet with him. He patted the back of her gloved hand and smiled. "I promise to return, Cory. And I promise to help." He leaned in, placing a kiss on her cheek and then whispering, "No harm will come to you on my watch. I will see to it."

And he left, taking the picture with him just as Flossie came running into the room out of breath. "Where did he go? Where did he go, Cory?"

Cory touched her cheek, the one Larkin had swept his lips across. "He went to fetch a book because he thinks he's seen the ring before."

"And you let him leave? Coriander!" She blew out a breath and tried to stomp her foot on the ground, but the carpet muffled her again. "He could be halfway to the police. We need to get to horse!"

"He kissed my cheek, Flossie, and now I feel like a thousand fireworks are going off in my stomach. What does that mean?"

"Uh-oh," was Flossie's only answer as Cory stood at the large window and waited for Larkin to come back so maybe she could ask him.

CHAPTER 17

"Cousin, you are in trouble in more ways than one." Flossie joined her at the window, laced her arm through the crook of Cory's elbow, and steered her toward the chair nearest the fireplace. "This conversation calls for tea and biscuits."

"Perhaps a slice of lemon cake." Cory glanced at the dainty package on the table, its ribbon coiled around it like a viper waiting to strike, and winced. "I find that I don't have a taste for biscuits at the moment."

Or that she ever would again for that matter.

"Yes, of course." Flossie followed her gaze to the package, her lips mashed together in a flat line, and nodded. "Lemon cake. And something stronger than tea, perhaps."

Lost in the tumultuous thoughts of murder, betrayal, the budding attraction she felt for one brooding and infuriating man, and the guilt that came with it,

Coriander sat in the chair oblivious to everything around her until she felt the weight of the diamond-cut cordial glass pressed into her hand.

"Sherry, for the nerves. No one seems to have seen anyone drop off the package. Not a single person saw it dropped off. Are we certain Mr. Reardon was not the one to bring it with him?" Flossie swept her hand behind her, shifting her skirts to one side, and perched on the edge of the chair opposite Cory. She took a sip from her glass and watched the flames consume the small stack of logs inside the fireplace.

Cory thought for a moment before answering. He had been there when she'd found the dead woman in the rookery. He'd also been in the box next to her at the opera. But had he been the one to bring her the cookie as a warning? Passing it off as a delivery when really he was the threat? In her heart she knew he was only here to help. She trusted her instincts and they told her that he was an ally not a murderer. "No, he wouldn't have done that to me. Originally, I would have suspected him but I do not anymore. He is here for a reason and I trust that reason is not to harm me."

"I'll follow your lead on this, just this once. You've always gone about things your own way. Even when we were children. I should have known you wouldn't need my help."

"For once, cousin, I have to disagree. I am very much in need of your help." Cory took a large sip of her sherry, welcoming the warmth that spread through her chest and down to her stomach from the alcohol and that it also soothed the pain that admission cost her.

She hated to rely on anyone. Regardless of what anyone thought about her marriage to Ezra, it was a partnership. To the eyes of society peering in on their union, she appeared to be as any other kept woman in London, but her magic wasn't the only thing that separated her from them. It was her independence. The one wedding gift her dearly departed husband gave her that she cherished above all others. Coriander ran her house and her life as she saw fit without question or consequence. Apart from her craft. And even then, she had the freedom to practice, to plant her gardens, grow her stores of potions, salves, and healing teas.

Just as Ezra had his freedom to travel and pursue his inventions. Something he appreciated from the start. One of Ezra's favorite qualities about Coriander had been her ability to take care of herself and their home in his absence. He reminded her of it whenever he answered the call of adventure and left Elmcroft in pursuit of his latest historical treasure.

"You've never once asked for help in all the days we have been married. Some might consider that a character flaw." Ezra's last words before he left for Egypt came back to her in a rush. She recalled the slight twitch in his lips at the pointed look she gave him for that teasing remark and the smile that replaced it with his next words. "But your independent nature is one of your best qualities. I think it's what drew me to you in the first place. All the men clamoring to scrawl their name on your dance cards, searching high and low when you were agreeable enough to play Sardines."

His lips curved up into a full smile then, softening his features and warming his eyes. He pulled her to him, his hands slid over her hips, and he wrapped his arms around her waist.

"You let me find you that day. Don't think I don't know it. My darling Coriander, you never wanted or needed someone to take care of you. The fact that you permit me is proof enough of your feelings for me. It gives me peace to know that I can leave you, to not worry that there is no one here to take care of you because you can take care of yourself." Ezra pressed his lips to hers and said goodbye for the last time.

Oh, but if he could see her now. Forced to ask for help from a man who unnerved her in the best and worst possible ways. She told Larkin that she had the means to finish this nasty business with whomever was responsible for the murders of her husband, his friend and hers—and she did.

But she couldn't do it alone.

Another painful admission. One that stirred another, more troubling thought from the memory of her last goodbye with Ezra. Had he known? Had he suspected the danger that awaited them, yet said nothing as he set off for his next adventure? She knew that his addiction to the possibility of a new discovery ran deep, but was it enough that he would cast those suspicions aside, risking his safety and hers? There was a finality to Ezra's words Coriander hadn't considered before.

"As for Mr. Reardon, I should have known you would be drawn to him the moment he stepped into the Havershalls' dining room. Your tastes have always been unconventional." Flossie sliced through her serving of lemon cake with her fork and took a healthy bite.

"I beg your pardon?" Cory feigned offense when in fact she was relieved to be pulled from her troubling thoughts by her cousin's unintentional slight.

Deciding it was best not to dwell on the timing of Ezra's revelation about his financier, she shoved those doubts to the back of her mind. It was better not to go down that road of thinking. No good would come of it. If Ezra had his suspicions, she could only assume he also had his reason for not sharing them with her before he left for Egypt.

"He's more than handsome enough to be a match for you, Cory. Which I suspect has something to do with those fireworks you described. But he is in the employ of a particular secret society whose life mission is to expose magic. Ezra was an adventurer and inventor."

Flossie pointed her finger toward the ceiling and the rooms beyond. More specifically the attic where they both knew Ezra's workshop resided and the last place they'd seen his spirit.

"As I said, Cory, unconventional. Still, your judgment has proven sound in the past, and I should not have doubted it now. As long as he makes you happy, cousin. It's been too long since you were. Larkin Reardon will challenge you. Something else you have been missing for too long. He is a good choice for you."

"I am plenty challenged by yet another murder investigation that I have found myself at the center of, and I haven't chosen anyone." Coriander wasn't as certain of that as she should have been. She feared that more than one part of her body may have made that decision for her. Though it most assuredly wasn't her brain.

"Ahem." Esther cleared her throat and rapped her knuckles on the frame of the entranceway. "Mr. Reardon to see you, ma'am."

Coriander wasn't positive, but she thought she heard an amused chuckle from Esther as she slipped behind Mr. Reardon and disappeared out into the hallway where she would no doubt continue to eavesdrop on the conversation.

In the time it had taken for cake to be plated, then served, along with the tea Esther insisted Cory and Flossie would want after they finished their sherry, Mr. Reason had returned. He had said he could ride to his lodgings and back faster than Cory could have a carriage prepared, but she hadn't expected him to be *that fast*.

"Mr. Reardon." Cory shot up from her chair, the embarrassment of what she assumed he overheard from the doorway heating her skin more than the flames in the fireplace at her back.

"After what we have conspired to do together, I insist you call me Larkin." The man couldn't have made the word *conspire* sound more scandalous if he tried.

That confirmed it. He had indeed overheard their conversation. Damn. She couldn't recall the last time she had been so out of sorts with herself. She blamed it on the murders—and not the dark-haired, dark-eyed, broad-shouldered man before her. Murders. Yes. That had to be it. Surely that was enough to throw any sensible witch off her broom.

Not that she rode one. She much preferred the comforts of a saddle or carriage.

"Then I insist you call me Cory." It seemed the sherry had loosened her tongue, unlike the corset cinched around her that constricted her lungs and made it impossible to draw a deep breath—or perhaps that had nothing to do with her undergarments and everything to do with Larkin Reardon.

"Cory." He rolled her name over his tongue, slow, as if tasting it, savoring it. "Hmm, if it's all the same to you, I prefer Coriander. I like the way it feels and sounds when I say it."

It surprised Coriander to find that she liked the way it felt and sounded when he said her name as well. Quite possibly, more than she should.

"Mr. Reardon, you've returned." Flossie pointed toward the soft leather-bound journal tucked under Larkin's arm. "And you found your book."

Once again, her cousin came to the rescue, swooping in with a much-needed distraction from the delicious tension that seemed to simmer in the air whenever Larkin was in the same room as Cory.

"As promised." Larkin's long legs made short work of crossing the room before freeing the book from beneath his arm. He joined Coriander and Flossie by the fireplace, his fingertips dancing along the edge of the pages until he came to the one with a scrap of paper to mark its place. "And I was correct, I have seen the ring you're looking for. Though I must confess, I wish I hadn't."

"But it's a lead, Mr. Rear—" Coriander caught herself—and the flick of gaze in her direction—before she fell back into formality. She also noted the shift of his lips and hint of a smile when she corrected herself and called him by his given name. "Larkin. Any lead is good news."

"On that we must agree to disagree." He flipped open the book, pressing along the inseam to flatten the spine, and tapped his finger beside an image similar to the one Cory had sketched, though the etchings and inscriptions were more detailed. "If you thought the organization I work for is secretive, we are a public commodity in comparison to the Order of the Hammer."

"The Order of the Hammer?" Coriander raised her hand to her mouth, her fingertips pressed against her lips in a failed attempt to stifle her gasp before it escaped. She shook her head, loosening what was left of the curls pinned on top of her head. "It's not possible."

"They disbanded. There has been no word of a resurgence within the community. Not even a whisper in a dark corner." Flossie grabbed her glass from the table, moved to the walnut-finished sideboard, plucked the stopper from the bottle, and refilled her glass with sherry before sinking down on the couch nearest the liquor cabinet. "Someone would have said. We would have known."

"Impossible. Ezra wouldn't have accepted money from them. Knowing who and what I am. *Knowing who they are.*" Cory refused to believe something so ill of her husband. "He would have sold Elmcroft to his brother to finance his expedition before aligning himself with anyone representing, or pretending to represent the Order."

"Coriander." Larkin reached for her, his hands gripping her forearms for a moment before, with a gentle shake, he released his hold and let her go. "I would never presume Ezra was in league with the order. Only that he wouldn't have known. Until it was too late."

"He would have warned me." Coriander forced the whispered words over the sob stuck in her throat, squeezing her eyes shut to stop the tears that threatened to spill over as she shook her head again. "No."

No. No. No. She wanted to scream the word at the top of her lungs. The denial of the truth was rooted so firmly in her heart and mind.

"Could he have? All the way from Egypt? If the Order had the smallest suspicion Ezra uncovered the truth about his financier, he would not have had the time to write a letter, much less send one." Larkin's tone was soft, patient and while he thwarted her attempt at denial with more logic, he hadn't clubbed her upside the head with it either. He spared her the harshest part of the truth and seemed to be trying his best to allow her to process their latest revelation on her own.

The lead she had been excited for only moments before.

"Then it's true. The special inspector was correct in his first assessment. I killed my husband." Cory felt her knees wobble beneath her and braced herself with her hand on the back of her chair.

"Cory," Flossie scolded, pushing to her feet on legs that wobbled from sherry and not from the proverbial world having been rocked beneath her feet like Coriander. "Don't listen to her, Mr. Reardon. The stress and the sherry have gone to her head. She was cleared of all charges. In the court and the community."

"Fear not, Flossie. I may not know Coriander well." Larkin tipped his head in her direction. "Something I intend to rectify post haste, but I do know she didn't kill her husband."

"I may as well have. I married him and that sealed his fate." Cory's grip on the back of the chair faltered, and for a moment she thought she might collapse. "You should go, Mr. Reardon. Lest you befall the same fate."

"Are we to be engaged then, Coriander? I believe it is customary for the man to propose," Larkin teased and then teased some more. "I must say, this is a bit unconventional, and yet I find myself inclined to accept."

Unconventional. There was that blasted word again. As much as it infuriated her, she could hardly deny the description fit. Nothing about her life or the circumstances she was in were conventional.

And they most certainly were not getting engaged.

CHAPTER 18

Cory paced along the carpet in the parlor. She was not going to deign to respond to his engagement comment. They were not, nor would they ever be, engaged in anything. Well, except for this newest wrinkle. Gods, the Order of the Hammer. As far as anyone in her circle knew they had closed years ago when the headmaster of the organization had taken his own life in an effort to harness energy and magic he had no business playing with and certainly not enough knowledge to possess.

And now, by some horrendous curse of fate, they were not only back but also in the vicinity and killing people. For what? Magic?

The answer was not new. It was one she'd thought of before and had wondered how or why they thought they could get it. But if the Order was involved, then they were dealing with something far more sinister and evil than she might be prepared to battle.

The image of her friend Kitty being put in the ground by the opening doors of the drop-bottom coffin sprang into Cory's head, unneeded but perhaps necessary. If someone had killed her and Havershall's wife to gain their magic then no one was safe, especially not anyone she cared for.

And if Ezra had somehow been involved with them, even if he had not known it until the bitter end, then she would deal with that later. It was done, whatever had led to her husband's death was done. She needed to focus to not meet up with him far sooner than she had hoped to.

"We must track down the Order," she said, thinking out loud. Perhaps she should have kept that thought to herself.

Flossie gasped and Larkin put his hand on her arm again. What else could she say to get him to keep it there this time?

Before she was ready, he released her and started pacing opposite to her. They'd go by each other every few feet once they turned around and passed back the other way. She paused when they met up and so did he, but then they both shook their heads and continued on.

Flossie watched them from her perch on the couch and then shook her head too and went back to eating her cake.

"If they are involved then we have bigger problems than I would have thought," she said, passing Larkin one more time before turning at the mantle.

"We cannot seriously be considering going up against the Order. They might have disbanded, but almost no organization is completely rendered dead even if its leader is gone."

"Did you think they were still operating?" Cory asked on their next passing.

Larkin shrugged and red tipped his ears.

"No," he grumbled. "No, I did not think they were in operation. They were meant to go down in the annals of history as a severely wrong turn and a tale of caution to scare children and men alike into behaving, similar to tales of the boogeyman, but worse."

"Yes," Flossie said, finally joining the conversation again. "Much worse."

Cory's eyes darted to her cousin, knowing that she was thinking of their great-great grandmother, who had been integral in the group's downfall though few people knew that. It was their own form of the boogeyman and one of the reasons that they had always been so careful to stay low-profile.

"Much, much worse." Larkin increased his speed and lapped Cory twice before she met him again in the middle. This time it was she who grabbed his arm. It was so strong and warm. The feel of him under her fingertips felt like a furnace being fired up.

When she went to snatch her hand back, he covered it with his own. They stared into each other's eyes and that flutter from before built into a swirl of the most turbulent sea roiling in her stomach. What was this feeling and why did she both loathe and yet crave it?

Flossie rose from the sofa and broke the spell Cory had felt wrapping around her with each second that passed looking deeply into Larkin's gold-flecked eyes.

Cory stepped back from Larkin, and he released his hold on her arm slowly by dragging his fingers down over her wrist and along the skin on the back of her hand. She'd never thought she was sensitive there, as she often had her hands in dirt or covered in pollen or any number of things when she was tending her plants. And she often had gloves on out in society. But that gentle brush was wreaking havoc on her system and she needed to get herself back under control. Now.

She did not resume her pacing as she didn't want to pass Larkin again and be tempted to reach out. So, she followed Flossie's lead and poured herself some more sherry. That might not have been the best idea, but it was a sight better than the thoughts that were running through her mind and what his feathery touch would feel like in other places.

Oh, she needed to get back on track.

She avoided the quizzical look Flossie was trying to pin her down with and took a dainty sip of her drink, allowing it to sear down her throat and bloom in her chest and belly. That was better.

"What do you know of the Order... Larkin?" She'd almost said Mr. Reardon but she did not want to show how much these last few moments had affected her.

He cleared his throat and seemed entranced by the view to the backyard.

"They had been around for decades and perhaps even centuries. Certain mythology and lore put them as descendants of the followers of the Egyptian god

Ptah. He was the creator god, a patron of craftsmen and architects. They sacrificed to him in order to be able to create bigger and better buildings and to bless those they had made to stand tall." He scratched his chin. "He was to be a benevolent god, but as every generation seems to do, some people turned him into a vengeful god and one that would require ultimate sacrifices to keep some safe while others must perish for the good of all, or at least everyone else." He chuckled but it sounded harsh, not mirthful at all. "Those who performed the sacrifices usually did so right before it would have been time to pay those who had labored day and night to bring the buildings, homesteads, and markets to life. Somehow that always seems to be the case."

"Indeed." Flossie was the one who took up the pacing this time and she gave Larkin a wide berth. He laughed briefly until she shot him a venomous glance.

"Pardon me," he said, bowing deeply at the waist.

"You are pardoned." She sniffed. "Now, the Order was one of the cornerstones of that civilization, but nearly every culture has some form. They existed and branched off in many directions from that original story."

Larkin nodded. "Indeed."

"And the one that had been very powerful in these parts was demolished when the leader fell, may he rot in the fiery depths."

Flossie almost snarled that last part, and Cory watched Larkin to see his reaction.

He simply kept looking in the back garden. What did he see out there? Her perfectly tended flowers? The wild growth of her deadly patch of earth, filled with all manner of things that could cut someone down in a blink? She only cultivated those in an effort to understand nature and to give honor to all plants no matter what their true purpose. Or did he just see a bunch of green and not understand what power she had at her very fingertips if she so chose to use it?

"And yet..." Larkin trailed off and pulled at the knot of his cravat. "And yet, we have heard some rumblings that would make so much more sense if the Order has been reborn."

"What do you mean?" Cory asked.

He cleared his throat. "There have been rumors that someone and something has been playing with a form of magic that should never have existed. One that was not meant to be used at all and yet fell into the wrong hands ages ago."

"What rumors? What magic?" Cory stepped closer and then stopped herself, not wanting to be too close.

"Just rumors." Larkin shrugged and raised his hands with his palms up, and Cory alternatively wanted to shout at him to spit it out and also rest her cheek on one of those palms.

She was being an idiot. Righting herself both in stature and attitude, she doubled down on her discipline, the kind that had made her capable of taking care of herself no matter the circumstance.

"We need more answers than that, Larkin. If you know something, then you must tell us. People are in danger, both my kind and the world in general if the Order is making a comeback and doing so by killing those with magic to harness and then use their powers. We're not dealing with a few unfortunate accidents here." Should she produce the recordings now that Flossie was back? Would it encourage him to come clean with them so that they all knew the same information? However, to be fair, it wasn't as if she had been telling the whole story of what she knew. Ezra's ghost and the others that had shared information with her were not something she was prepared to divulge completely.

He drew in a breath and seemed to fortify himself. "There is a reason that I am part of the Society of Paraphysical Research."

Cory waited for him to continue, and Flossie leaned in as if that would make him finish his thought.

"Yes. And?"

"There is a reason I belong to the Society."

"You've already said that." What was he getting at and why was it taking him so long to be out with it?

"The reason is that I believe my family is descendants of that very man who killed himself in pursuit of power, and I will not have the horrors that happened then happen now. There is chaos in allowing one man to have that much power, and it bled out through my family over these many generations. I will put an end to it and keep people safe from all the wicked ways in which a single man plays with so many people's lives like some kind of puppet master with all the marionette strings in his hands."

The ferocity nearly radiated out of Larkin. It was a vast difference to the way he normally seemed to have convictions but would also flow from one thing to the next as if nothing truly bothered him and this was all a big game.

He'd been hurt, and Cory for some unknown reason suddenly wanted to know exactly why and how so that she could use her herbs and magic and potions to smite whoever would have done something like this to him.

"What information do you have that the Order has begun to recruit and be active again?"

Larkin moved closer to the windows and braced a hand on the sill, leaning forward so far that his forehead rested against the pane of glass.

"We have heard people talk about sacrifices that have been made, whispers in dark corners asking if finally, the magic will once again rule the world. That it will no longer have to hide in the dark because people do not or will not understand the power to be had. The power with all the benefits inherent in being able to create emotions and riches and standing with a few words and a burning candle."

Flossie scoffed. "Magic is not that simple, and neither is it that powerful. There is so much that would need to come into alignment to be able to make those kinds of changes within our world and the world at large."

"And yet," Cory said, "And yet, are they not moving toward that? Killing various women who would have the power to snap their fingers and make a person choke on their own air? Yes, in the normal sphere of our world that would come with consequences three-fold that the user would not be able to survive. But if they are bottling it, Flossie. If they are making it so that the magic is extracted into a thing and then used in a ritual to serve a new master. A master who does not have to say those words but can then reap all the benefits of the spell. Is that not what they are doing?"

Oh, how she wished she could talk to Ezra and see if there was anything more he had found out before he'd been killed. Who was the man who had talked to him in that recording? Had they killed Ezra because he would not go along with their scheme? And how did Larkin tie into all of this? Because Cory had a distinct feeling that he knew far more than he was letting on.

Part of her wanted ask if he knew the sender of the biscuit. And the other part was very much afraid that she might be looking at that answer right now as he rested his forehead against the cool pane of glass.

Were any of Larkin's current family members some of the original Order and that's why he was so adamant to not fall into the trap and protect those who were being abused?

CHAPTER 19

Coriander reached for the letter that had accompanied the funeral biscuit, an idea forming in her mind. Though she had no desire to study the handiwork of the baker who scrawled her initials in icing over the biscuit, the contents of the letter were another matter entirely.

"I'm inclined to accept this invitation." Her lips mashed into a fine line, and her brows pinched together as she mulled over the correspondence laced with threats.

"Excuse me?" Flossie sputtered, choking on the tea she had just switched to, then dabbed at the corners of her mouth with a linen napkin.

"This can't possibly come as a surprise to you," Cory teased. Her cousin knew her best of all. If anyone could predict Coriander's next move it would be Flossie.

Whether she supported Cory's decisions was another matter entirely.

"A surprise?" Flossie scoffed, setting her tea on the mahogany side table with a forceful hand, rattling the bottom of the porcelain cup against its saucer. "The inclination to accept, no. The sheer lack of common sense and self-preservation in doing so, yes."

"It makes quite a bit of sense, cousin, if you stop and think about it." Coriander followed the creases in the paper, folding it back into a neat square before tucking it into the pocket of her dress, then returned to pacing the floor in front of the fire. The idea might not be the smartest at this point, but she needed to be doing something. She'd been threatened, and this person was not going to quit until he was forced to cease his dastardly deeds. This would end with her, one way or another.

"You haven't stopped to think at all."

Cory's spine stiffened as she came to a halt before the fireplace. She would not look at Flossie, who most likely thought her words had the desired effect. Cory did not want to see the look of grim satisfaction that her cousin probably wore. No one was going to stop her, she'd merely paused to solidify her plan, that was all.

"You must know this is a trap, Coriander." Larkin stepped toward her, closing the small distance between them.

Between her focus on attending Timothy's funeral and his silence, she had almost forgotten Larkin was there. A near-impossible feat with him at her side. He smelled of scotch and bergamot, with a hint of the smoke from the fire and stable from his ride earlier.

The mix of scents were heady, masculine, and utterly distracting.

As was the graze of his fingertips against her hip when he moved in front of her, blocking her view of the flames and the warmth of the fire with his broad shoulders and back.

Larkin took a step to her left, and then another and another until she felt the weight of his presence at her back. And then it was gone. She felt his absence immediately and was surprised by the wave of loss and longing that washed over her. The rustle of paper, somehow louder than the crackling wood inside the hearth, drew her from the flames to the alluring man who had picked her pocket. Scoundrel! But despite the skillful effort, his larcenist act had not gone unnoticed.

And yet, she'd allowed it.

"You will want to attend... I will be there also... It would only take one word for your entire world to change, and I'm prepared to speak that one word." Larkin picked lines from the letter with the same deftness he had picked her pocket, but he was not as proficient in masking the emotion in his voice. "Signed the Rook."

"The Rook," Coriander repeated and met Larkin's gaze. That was the final word on the letter. "A nod to the location of his first murder. A nice touch. Sentimental, if not a bit heavy-handed."

"Perhaps," he said glaring at the letter before snapping his eyes back up to her.

Larkin's dark, piercing eyes burned with a cold passion that left her soul both seared and frostbitten. The unadulterated rage she saw should have frightened her, but she knew those feelings weren't meant for her but for the man who threatened her.

"Though I suspect it refers to the pieces that remain on his gameboard. This is his final move. The Rook believes he's checked his king. Your presence at that funeral all but secures his victory," Larkin said in a voice that caused her to take a step back.

But then she stepped forward again. She was not going to let someone play with her life, or anyone else's, anymore. "I may be under attack, Larkin, but there are other pieces left on the board. I am not unprotected, and I will not be captured," Cory snapped. She knew it was in response to the underlying implication that as if by her feminine nature she was weak and defenseless, but she couldn't stop herself. She was tired of feeling helpless. She paused as a dangerous thought slithered its way through her mind. It crossed a line, exposing herself and her magic in a way she never had before. Not even with Ezra. "Or perhaps you'd care to join me for a walk in my garden where I can show you how well-defended I truly am."

"I am well aware of the species tended in your garden, Ms. Whitlock." One corner of Larkin's mouth curved into a wry smile as he arched a brow—as if in challenge to the fact that she had not poisoned him already.

Something she questioned on more than one occasion after she found him lurking by her garden gate and all but forced his way into her house, and then questioned further after the first stirrings of attraction to a man who should for all intents and purposes be off limits to her because of the secret society who employed him.

She refused to examine the true reason too closely.

"My concern for your wellbeing has nothing to do with your capabilities." Larkin's expression changed again, the laugh lines at the corners of his mouth and eyes smoothed away once he schooled his features. "Your safety is of the utmost importance to me. Despite my best efforts not to, I worry. I am compelled to look after you. If I didn't know better, I would think I'd been bespelled."

Coriander's gaze shifted to the chair occupied by her cousin, who had remained uncharacteristically quiet during their exchange.

"Don't look at me, cousin." Flossie's hands were raised, palm out, in front of her in a placating gesture. "If it were my compulsion spell, he wouldn't know what hit him."

"I'm sure the inspector would agree. That would certainly explain his peculiar behavior when he discovered Coriander covered in blood at the scene of the crime."

Cory ignored Larkin's knowing wink and matching grin. But then his focus settled once again on Coriander. She wanted to point out that the inspector wouldn't have found her at all if he hadn't directed him there in the first place. She considered the argument as a possible distraction from her plan to attend the funeral but knew Larkin was a man of conviction and would not be deterred.

"As to the matter at hand," he continued, "the pursuit of the Rook, perhaps we could evaluate alternative options and save the one most likely to end with you in peril as a last resort?"

"Continue to underestimate my capabilities, Mr. Reardon, and you will be the one in peril." Coriander's light tone belied the truth of her words. She was not a violent woman or a witch who thumbed her nose at the creed, but she was tired of the death that surrounded her and intended to put a stop to it.

While she wouldn't add to the number of bodies at the morgue, she knew of more than one way to make Larkin's life uncomfortable—many of which grew right outside her kitchen window.

"If I underestimated your skills, Coriander Whitlock, I would not have gone to such great lengths to meet you. I don't call upon every midwife, alchemist or spiritualist listed amongst the names the society has collected." Larkin followed the creases in the card stock, folded the letter and tucked it in his jacket pocket. A wry smile curved one corner of his mouth, as if he was certain she wouldn't dare attempt to retrieve it.

"No, it would seem that honor is reserved for me and Madam Olivia." Coriander's fingers itched with the need to reach into his pocket and snatch the letter. It was addressed to her after all, her property, but she refused to give him the satisfaction.

"I already told you why I was there." Larkin's voice deepened to rich, velvet bass and his eyes darkened. The flash of danger she saw in their obsidian depths was for an entirely different reason than the one implied in the correspondence tucked away in his jacket pocket.

"Ahem." Flossie cleared her throat, a much-needed reminder that Coriander and Larkin were not alone in her parlor. Her cousin was not one to fade into the background and was not accustomed to being ignored.

She ruled her house and if she had her way, Coriander's love life as well— and she felt certain that Larkin was not the type of match Flossie intended to make, no matter what she had said earlier. "Perhaps we could focus on the madman running loose on London, killing witches and calling himself the Rook, considering he has now set his sights on Coriander."

"Yes, Flossie dear, of course. You're right, as usual." A little flattery never hurt where her cousin was concerned. Coriander knew to soften her up, the same way she would the hardened earth before planting any seed in her garden. Though this particular idea would take every ounce of her magic to take root and grow in the stubborn minds of two of her most trusted confidants.

It surprised her to realize how effortless it had been for Larkin to claim such a position in her life. The question that remained was whether or not he could hold on to it. Before Ezra, it had been her experience that few people ever could. It surprised her further to realize she hoped Larkin would prove to be the exception and not the rule.

"So, you agree that this Rook is dangerous and you should—" Flossie's relief sputtered away upon her cousin's interruption.

"Come up with a plan. I couldn't agree more, Flossie." Coriander met her cousin and Larkin's confounded expressions with a stiff spine and confident gaze. "How fortunate am I to have the two of you to strategize with."

"For the love of the goddess, Coriander Whitlock, you know that is not what I was about to say." Flossie shuttered her eyelids and pinched the bridge of her nose as she let out an exasperated sigh.

"There is no way I can dissuade you from attending this funeral, is there?" Larkin's concern was evident in the strain of his voice, the crease formed between his brows, and the downward turn of his mouth. He must have seen the determination in Coriander's face when he looked at her, because he shook his head and forced his beautiful lips into a neutral position. Not quite a smile, but a concession nonetheless.

Coriander wasn't one to beg for scraps, but in that moment, she would take what she could get.

"The Rook is thinking two moves ahead. He's confident he'll win this game. You know what that means." Larkin closed the distance between them, and Cory found her eyes leveled with his chest as he towered over her. "But you should also know the lengths that I will go to prevent that from happening."

Coriander's heart hammered in her chest, beating against her ribs in a wild attempt to break free of its cage, and there was a slight tremor in her hand as she rested her palm against his chest, her fingers curled beneath the lapel of his coat. "I do, Larkin. Thank you."

If the groundskeeper were to dig another grave, Coriander knew without a doubt it would not be hers. She trusted Larkin, he was a man of his word. She knew that. She also knew what it would cost him to keep it.

She would do everything in her power to ensure he never paid that price.

CHAPTER 20

Planning and strategizing needed far more than some biscuits and tea, or even a glass of sherry. Cory pulled Esther aside to prepare a meal that could be served while they talked and laid out what would need to happen at the funeral tomorrow. A part of her was completely terrified by the prospect of being in a place where she knew without a shadow of a doubt that she could be in the crosshairs of someone's desire to harm her. The other side of her shoved that trepidation away and stood tall. This killer had no idea who he was messing with but if she had anything to do with it, he was about to find out.

Conversation was sparse and stilted while they waited for the food to be set out. Cory turned several times, thinking to end the awkward and heavy silence that permeated the room, but she didn't know what to say, and she wasn't sure she was actually going to eat.

So much hung in the balance right now. Her mind kept going back and forth between the women who had suffered and died and her husband before them and now Timothy. She had loved him as her husband's best friend for years, until her husband was killed and he tried to pin it on her so that the authorities wouldn't look at him.

And now she had to follow a trail of breadcrumbs that she felt Ezra's automated floor sweeper was sucking up before she could get a grip on what they meant. She knew why these particular women, at least at the core. The first two had some kind of magic. Because of Ezra's recordings she knew that the deaths were for magic and now they also knew it had to do with the Order of the Hammer. Kitty and Timothy were then death by association. But what were they missing that would tell them the name of the scoundrel? How was she supposed to find a man with a particular ring on his finger? Who would he try to take next? And how could she ask without showing her hand or spotlighting women who like her wouldn't want the world at large to be aware of her powers?

She still had tenuous ties to many of the powerful in the area, but years ago they had stopped meeting in groups for fear that they would be caught and questioned and ultimately killed. Fortunately, she had Flossie to talk with but not all the other women had anyone much less a coven to turn to if things were tough.

And knowing that Larkin and his kind were out there looking for them didn't help. She shouldn't be attracted to him. She shouldn't want to know what those fingers would feel like if they went above her wrist or happened to brush more than just her hip.

A blush worked its way up her neck. She was never so thankful to see Esther roll in one of Ezra's automatic carts with a display of meats and cheeses accompanied by sauces and a loaf of her flaky and divine bread. She used the herbs from Cory's garden out back—the one that didn't have plants that would kill you if you tried to ingest them.

Larkin looked at the bread and then looked at her, and she couldn't help but let one side of her mouth kick up in a mischievous half-smile. Let him wonder. For her part, she was going to dive in so she had enough sustenance to make all the stops she planned on making in the next several hours.

Asking Larkin to accompany her back to the Havershalls' but stay in Flossie's carriage had taken some very fancy waltzing through a dialogue where he seemed more perplexed than irritated, but she'd managed to do it. Keeping Flossie in the carriage or where Cory really wanted her, back at Elmcroft, had been shot down immediately with some threats and a few nasty words.

Once Cory gave in though, Flossie was as pleasant as the tea they'd all had after finishing off the meats and cheeses. Cory knew she could have given her some kind of sleeping agent—she'd had one up her sleeve for the last three hours—but in the end she just hadn't been able to do it. Not to mention that she would have had hell to pay when Flossie woke up and that wasn't worth ever doing something like that when you were dealing with a woman who could lure you into dancing a jig, naked as the day you were born, down the street and cackling the whole time. She'd almost done it once to a solicitor who had only been trying to collect on a debt that Flossie's husband had not yet paid, but Flossie had had no problem sending the man on his way with a promise to pay as soon as she wanted to. Her husband had barely talked her out of it and now she used far more caution in her magical dealings.

And so now they stood in the foyer of the Havershalls' home, waiting for their card to be received and hopefully to be ushered into the drawing room. She had confirmed that the elder Havershall was in court session before heading here as she did not want to see him after he'd forced her to attend the opera and be accosted by Timothy Revelson. She only wanted to be here when the odious man was not.

Her thoughts immediately went back to the night of the séance. So much had happened. She'd almost exposed her ability to speak with the dead by boosting the energy for the counterfeit medium to be able to give true and accurate information from the deceased, which had then led to that spirit attaching itself to her and following her to then possessing her. Fortunately, she'd been able to cut the ties but the woman's words, the wife of the younger Mr. Havershall, had continued to haunt her long after the ghost and passed on. What did it all mean? And how did meeting Larkin seem to have changed everything in not only her life but in her feelings?

Fortunately, she was interrupted by the butler before she could go too deep down that particular rabbit hole. It served no purpose to overanalyze things that had little to nothing to do with finding the killer. At this point that was her one and only purpose. Everything else could wait.

"Behave yourself in here," Flossie whispered from beside her as Cory nearly marched into the drawing room. She was pulled back and forced to slow down by Flossie as she had nearly overtaken the butler and rushed right past him.

That would not do. She had to keep her head on straight and focus solely on her purpose here. Being confrontational would help no one.

"Coriander and Flossie, what a delight to have you visit."

Cory rolled her eyes as Flossie jabbed her with an elbow. Cory was certain that the younger Mr. Havershall was a nice enough person, but she had no need for him or for his platitudes. He stood to the side of the fireplace, leaning on it with his hands behind his back. If he fell there'd be no way he'd catch himself before his face hit the marble fireplace. That too was not of consequence at the moment. He whisked a quick hand through his slightly disheveled hair, and the sunlight hit the strands like a benediction, glinting for just a moment before Cory turned toward their hostess.

"Thank you so much for seeing us, madame. I appreciate your time." Cory slowed her words and blocked the ones that wanted to come crashing out of her mouth like a steam train. That would not serve the purpose she was here for.

Mrs. Havershall reclined on a striped couch and did not seem inclined to even sit upright for their visit. That would make it easier for Cory to feel like she could leave after a short time, so she said nothing.

"Of course, of course. And thank you so much for your presence the other night. It was a delight to see you even though the occasion was somber."

And then it had been scary, but she certainly couldn't say that to the old woman.

"Very somber. I just wanted to thank you for the invitation that night. I had not been to an event such as that and it was very interesting to see how your medium was able to make contact beyond the veil. Is she a friend of yours?"

"Ah, she is one of the best in the country and yes, a friend of mine. She has insight on so many things, and we always appreciate her sharing that insight with us."

For a price, Cory thought, and whatever that price was it was too much for the charlatan to ask. "Does she often contact the dead for you? Will she do it for others?"

"Are you wanting to contact your dear Ezra? I could certainly ask her to do that for me as a favor. She would be most willing, I'm sure."

Cory fought hard not to let her disgust show on her face. She could contact him and actually contact him for real without a fraud's help. But it was as good a story as any and explained better why she would be asking than her lame attempt at coming here just to thank the hostess. "That would of course be lovely if you would be so inclined to ask."

Flossie coughed at Cory's elbow, but she ignored her.

"Do you know if she has other friends who do the same thing? I'd heard that there was a disturbance recently with several people who have powers similar to hers coming to an awful demise. I hope she's safe. I wouldn't want to call her out where someone with ill intent could find her."

Mrs. Havershall scoffed. "She can protect herself. I will keep your card and have her contact you. I'm sure she'd be happy to reach across the veil to see if Ezra has any last words for you."

Cory smiled demurely because there was no way she'd be able to smile for real. She hooked her arm through Flossie's and led her out into the hall, not waiting for the butler this time. She knew her way out and couldn't stay in the woman's presence another second without wanting to yell about her complete incompetence and the way she was endangering others.

"Did you see the way the young Mr. Havershall flinched when you talked about the demise of people with powers?" Flossie asked. "I wonder what that was about?"

"Perhaps he knew his wife had powers of some sort and he is now wondering if that was the reason she died. That would be a hard pill to swallow if your family does not know the whole truth and you can't tell them without ruining everything."

"Should we tell Larkin?" Flossie paused on the front steps as the large door to the residence closed behind them.

As if he'd been waiting for their return, which he probably had, Larkin peeked his head out of the enclosed carriage. "You'd better tell Larkin everything or this goes no further."

Entering the carriage, Cory let Flossie tell of what had transpired in the drawing room of the Havershalls. Why had the younger Havershall flinched? Was it due to bringing up his wife and her death? Did he know what her powers were? Per her ghost, Coriander had gotten the impression that he had, but that was only an assumption on her part. There were many people within the craft who did not share anything of that magnitude with their husbands, simply wanting to be seen as coming from a high-born family but without the baggage of telling their husband of their abilities. Many who wanted to just be normal and forget that they had been born as far more than the average person. Cory judged none of them. Everyone had to make their own decisions. But how was the killer finding these women and how was he able to tell that they had a single ounce of magic in their blood?

The carriage had been moving while Flossie had talked Larkin's ear off. They hadn't talked about anything Cory didn't already know, so she paid little attention to their words. And that was why she knew exactly when they passed into the seedier part of town. It wasn't a far distance but the landscape and falling-down buildings made it look as if it were on a different planet. The streets were crowded and the carriage slowed to a crawl. Other streets must have been more open as she heard horses clattering along the cobblestones in a way they weren't on this street.

The buildings were in desperate need of repair, and the very air smelled foul enough to make Cory's eyes water. People yelled at each other from upstairs windows and shouted insults at each other on the sidewalks.

A whole other world. And she could have been caught here if she had not been found by Ezra and then loved by Ezra. She could have been Franny if her fortunes had fallen out from under her and she'd had no other choice.

The thought made her shiver.

Trundling through the Rookery made her think again of the letter that had been left in the box with the funeral biscuit. Was she ready to face down the person who had destroyed so many pieces of her life? What would she do when she faced him?

She did not know, but first she'd have to find him.

When they drew to a stop at the correct building, she was not surprised to see Franny's black-haired friend out on the street making eyes at every man who passed by. Cory could not call them gentlemen. She just couldn't.

Alighting from the carriage, Larkin was close behind her and she knew somewhere in her stomach and chest that there was no way he would be talked into staying with the carriage in this part of town. So, she didn't fight. But she did take the lead. Franny's friend got a hat-tip from Larkin but nothing else.

As she ascended the stairs, she shook off the intense feeling of dread and sadness as she moved toward the last place she'd seen Franny's other friend Kitty and where she'd been looking for anything to make this all make sense. But it never had, and maybe she might have to consider that it never would. But she wasn't giving up.

Moving up the last few stairs, she realized that she should have considered that Franny's room would not have been left empty after she'd died. The noises going on behind the thin wood door made her blush even as they also left her not knowing what on earth could be going on back there.

And then none of it mattered as she saw a note folded in half speared to the door frame with a letter opener. The end of the small sword-looking implement was emblazoned with a hammer and the one word scrawled on the front of the paper was her name in a script that was now all too familiar to her.

CHAPTER 21

"If I didn't know better, I would say the Rook has grown fond of you." Larkin gripped the handle of the silver letter opener, the muscles in his arm flexing as he tugged it free from the wooden door. "They say there is a fine line between love and hate."

"Who says?" Coriander kept her tone light despite the weight of their conversation and potential subject matter of the unopened letter in Larkin's hand. At every turn, the Rook remained one step ahead of them, anticipating their every move. Something that infuriated her to no end. "I think it is safe to say his feelings toward me remain the latter and the only thing the Rook is fond of is the idea of ridding himself of me once and for all."

She arched her brow, an expectant look in her eye, as she extended her hand and waited for Larkin to pass her the letter.

"Which is not going to happen." He ground out the words through clenched teeth. The muscle in his jaw twitched, a physical tell that she had become all too familiar with whenever Larkin struggled to maintain control of his emotions—in this case anger.

Though if she were honest with herself, it was anger or frustration in most cases that concerned Coriander. Perhaps that fine line between love and hate that Larkin spoke of came from personal experience.

Coriander took note of the texture of the paper as she unfolded the letter. Even through her gloved hand she felt its thickness, its weight, and knew it was of quality. The same quality of the calling cards used by the ton and not the poor souls residing in London's rookeries. Not that the observation should have surprised her. Men who joined the ranks of secret societies tended to be princes, not paupers.

"I believe this is nearing check. Your move, Ms. Whitlock. Signed, the Rook." Coriander knew he was taunting her, baiting her to ensure she attended Timothy's funeral. That knowledge did little to quell the tide of anger swelling within her. She crumpled the note into a ball and stuffed it into her reticule. She spared a glance at Larkin who, based on his strained expression, seemed poised to offer another warning about her attendance at the memorial service. "Not a word, Larkin. I'm going and that is final."

A loud thump and crash from the other side of the door stopped the disagreement they'd already had in her parlor from rekindling.

"You don't suppose?" Flossie moved between them, leaning against the door and pressing her ear to the wooden panel.

"The Rook is a methodical man. He wouldn't be so careless, not when he believes he's so close to achieving his goal." Larkin reached for Flossie, but she shrugged him off before his hand found purchase on her shoulder.

"Love and hate aren't the only opposites with a fine line between them, Mr. Reardon." Flossie wrapped her fingers around the doorknob in a white-knuckled grip.

Coriander's cheeks warmed at her cousin's insinuation but she tamped down the flush of embarrassment when she realized what Flossie actually meant—that a woman on the other side of that door wasn't held in throes of passion but the grip of a madman. While she didn't agree, she could understand the connection and her cousin's concern.

"There is a better chance of finding the Ripper behind that door than the Rook, Flossie." Larkin shook his head but made no further move to stop her from intruding on the private affairs of whoever was behind the door.

Flossie held her grip on the doorknob with one hand and rapped the knuckles of the other against the wood. "That may be true, but I'd rather be wrong than regretful."

"Wait your turn." A rough and scratchy voice barked in response from the other side of the thin walls.

"See, Flossie. Everything is fine... Well, not fine..." Coriander winced, struggling for the right words to explain the predicament of standing in the hall unintentionally eavesdropping on the business transaction happening on the other side of the door.

"You don't think he'd just announce himself, do you?" Flossie scoffed, turned the doorknob, and pushed open the door.

Coriander supposed her cousin had a point. If they had somehow arrived before the Rook made his escape, he certainly wouldn't alert them to his presence.

Flossie's fears were quickly allayed when the open door revealed the new tenant in Franny's apartment and her so-called gentleman caller.

"Oh, my apologies. As you were." Flossie stuttered, cheeks reddened in a shade of embarrassment that rarely made an appearance on her face, as she backed up into Larkin and slammed the door shut. "We should return to Elmcroft. We can't attend a funeral dressed like this."

Larkin offered Coriander his arm, escorting her behind her flustered cousin, out of the dilapidated tenement and to the carriage that awaited them.

Esther greeted them at the door, relieving them of their coats as she ushered them into the parlor before pouring each of them a glass of sherry. When she was satisfied everyone had been served and settled, she poured a glass for herself, tipped it back, swallowing the liquor in one gulp and then poured herself another.

In all the years she served this house, Coriander had not seen Esther drink more than one glass, and that was only on special occasions. She braced herself for whatever it was that Esther felt she needed the false courage alcohol provided to say.

"I won't stay here and wait to pick up the pieces again, Coriander. I can't. So, please, don't ask that of me."

Esther set the crystal decanter down on the bar top and her glass on the silver tray beside it.

"Oh, Esther." Coriander set her glass on the round table beside her chair, rose to her feet, and rushed to Esther's side. She'd been a devoted member of Elmcroft's staff, but more than an employee, she had been Coriander's friend, picking up the pieces after Ezra died. She couldn't imagine life without Esther in it, but she couldn't expect her to suffer through the potential loss of another Whitlock. "I wouldn't dare ask it of you. Once was enough. More than enough. The carriage is at your disposal. Henry will see you safely to your destination, wherever that may be."

"Coriander Whitlock." Esther scolded, her cheeks flushed with emotion. "After all these years, you of all people should know my character better than that. I am not abandoning you. I am coming with you."

"Oh, my sweet, loyal Esther." Coriander closed the distance between them and clasped their hands together. "I would never ask that of you. I couldn't bear the thought of something happening to you."

"I wasn't asking permission, Coriander." Esther raised her chin and straightened her spine, pushing her shoulders back, and stood at her full height.

The difference was small, but enough that Coriander was forced to incline her head if she wanted to meet Esther's fierce gaze. It was the first time in all her years at Elmcroft that Esther had refused a request—direct or implied—from Coriander. While her peers would have been enraged over such blatant insubordination, it only endeared Esther to her that much more

"Of course, you weren't." Coriander gave her hands a strong, reassuring squeeze before she released them and shifted the course of the conversation with a resounding clap. "Right then, we all have a funeral to attend. Time to dress the part."

It was said that misery loved company, and that had never been more evident than in London's love of funerals. Draped in the gloom of an overcast sky and the despair of the onlookers that lined the streets to watch the procession roll by, the city welcomed death into its bosom once more. Coriander, Flossie, Esther, and Larkin were pressed against each other, filling the small coach to capacity as Henry navigated the cobbled streets and slow-moving traffic ahead of them as they brought up the rear.

The Rook had claimed his last victim. It was time to put this nightmare to rest, once and for all. The cemetery was as inappropriate as it was a fitting location.

A funeral mute stood vigil at the gates to welcome mourners to the final resting place of the deceased, his sorrow and silent sobs bought and paid for with the few coins in his pocket and gin in his hand.

Coriander nodded at Larkin and then Flossie. The time had come for them to go their separate ways. Each had a part and position to fill in their plan to catch the Rook. Larkin strolled along the edge of the cemetery, sticking to the shadows where Coriander suspected he had been more comfortable before their paths had crossed. As sentinel, he would watch from the periphery for the Rook to make his move—a position he insisted Henry would be better suited for. Larkin argued to remain at Coriander's side, but conceded in the end when he failed to convince anyone in their party, himself included, that the Rook would make his presence known if he were beside her. Henry and Esther remained with the coach as the last line of defense should the Rook slip their grasp.

Coriander looped her arm through Flossie's, hooking them at the elbow as they strolled past the stone walls and through the wrought-iron gate into the cemetery toward the crowd gathered around a mound of fresh turned earth and a rectangular hole in the ground.

"Flossie." Coriander hissed, tightening her grip on her cousin's arm as she steered them off to the right and a distance away from the mourners gathered around the grave.

"What, what is it? Do you see something? Is it him?" Flossie's questions tumbled from her mouth in a rush. "The Rook?"

"Worse," Coriander grumbled, her irritation bubbling up at the oversight. "The inspector."

They should have expected Parker to make an appearance at the funeral. Though she suspected the inspector was there for closure rather than to offer condolences. After having wasted so much time investigating her for Ezra's murder, to then find and bring charges against the guilty party, only to have the long-awaited conviction overturned, she felt certain

Special Investigator Parker needed to see Revelson laid to rest—along with his part in Ezra's murder.

She chastised herself for not accounting for it.

"Damn." Flossie cursed the inspector's presence and reached into her reticule cinched around her wrist.

"Whatever is going round that head of yours, cousin, put a stop to it." Coriander wrapped her fingers around Flossie's wrist, applying enough pressure to force her cousin's hand to open. "No magic. Not until we know how the Rook is containing it. We need to split up."

"Are you mad?" Flossie hissed, eyes widened with disbelief at Coriander's suggestion. "Split up? Why don't you just truss yourself up like a turkey and offer yourself up on a silver platter? We are not making this easier for the murderous toss-pot."

Coriander couldn't help but smile at her cousin's colorful language. Flossie's status within the ton required a tight rein be kept on her emotions. The woman rarely, if ever, lost her manners in the company of her peers. And despite Revelson having been marked as a murderer, the man was a member of society and more than one person within their shared social circle felt compelled to attend the service.

Though Coriander suspected their compulsion had been fueled by the need to gossip rather than grieve.

"We're less conspicuous apart than together and we cannot afford to draw the inspector's eye. Not yet." Coriander let her gaze drift from her cousin to a quick survey of the cemetery grounds. "Parker mustn't find out about the Rook's true purpose. The murders, yes. The magic? No."

"Obviously." Flossie's tone was flat and her eyes narrowed as she folded her arms over her chest and waited for Coriander to elaborate on the evolution of their plan to trap the Rook.

"Right, then. You take the west wing and I'll veer off here toward the east wall." Coriander pointed toward the mausoleums and the crumbling stone wall on her right. "We will meet in the middle on the north side of the grounds. Be sure to bring Larkin up to speed when you cross paths."

"If Larkin is on the west wall, why don't you venture that way yourself?" Flossie pursed her lips and arched a quizzical brow at her cousin. "Because you know that with Special Inspector Parker here, he'll try and talk you out of this foolhardy plan?"

"Obviously." Coriander matched her cousin's tone and demeanor, arching a brow of her own in challenge. "This is the best plan we have. Unless of course you thought of something brilliant on the carriage ride over that you failed to share with the rest of us?"

Flossie mashed her lips into a thin line and to Coriander's relief said nothing. She let out the breath she'd been holding in anticipation of an argument that never came.

Coriander pulled her into a brief hug then pushed her away and peeled off down a narrow, worn path between a row of headstones on her right. Though the two often clashed heads, and Flossie drove her to the brink of insanity by meddling in her affairs, she couldn't imagine her life without the overbearing woman at her side. She paused long enough to cast a backward glance over her shoulder and toss a plea of caution to Flossie. "Be careful, cousin."

"I'm not the one the Rook is after. *You be careful*, Coriander."

And with that they headed off in opposite directions, but with a singular purpose. To flush out the Rook. Coriander welcomed the bit of fear that prickled her spine and raised goosebumps along her skin. To deny it would have been foolish and no doubt lead to reckless mistakes. Coriander wasn't rash. She was ready.

It was time for the Rook to pay for his sins, and she was there to collect.

CHAPTER 22

Roaming cemeteries was not new to Coriander. She'd spent plenty of time in the solemn and usually quiet resting places for the dead. Between learning her craft and being drawn to the afterlife of those who had gone before her, she knew the paths and alcoves of this place like she knew her own garden. Every stone, every mausoleum and crypt.

Ezra had sometimes chided her about spending more time with the dead than the living, but he'd always understood that here she could soak in the atmosphere and breathe in a way she had not been truly able to breathe until her garden at home flourished after years of taking care of it.

Now, she only wished to be done with this business of murder and treachery because no matter where she was, she couldn't seem to breathe right, even here.

And that was why she was not completely taken off guard when a force heavier than any she'd ever felt before dragged her into a mausoleum to her right. She'd wondered if the Rook would want this to be the place where they finally came face to face. Most likely he thought that he would be in control of everything and be able to control her with whatever magic he'd siphoned off the poor women who'd done nothing wrong except exist in this world.

He was about to find out how very wrong he was on several fronts.

She let the energy draw her through the open mausoleum door and didn't flinch when it slammed shut behind her. No matter what she was about to face, she was not afraid. He'd chosen the second to last best place to do this. Her garden would have been the ultimate destination of his undoing, but this particular cemetery was just as good.

Unfortunately, when she finally could look upon him, he had a mask on. An Egyptian pharaoh's golden face looked back at her in the dimly lit chamber. One from Ezra's collection, if she wasn't mistaken, and if anything, that only made her clench down harder on her will to win, no matter who this was.

"Interesting that you felt the need to pull me in with the very magic you've been hoarding. Afraid you wouldn't be able to physically manhandle a small, little woman like myself?" She was fully aware it probably would not help her cause to goad him, but after all she'd been through and all he'd done, she didn't give a rat's ass, to put it bluntly.

He merely shook his head and pulled a glowing burgundy bottle from the recesses of his jacket. Who was he? She stared hard trying to find any similarities to someone she knew, someone who had the will and the abilities to kill but also to funnel off the energy. Someone who would not be suspected of evil deeds until after they were already in progress.

A member of the police? She'd seen the inspector and several of his subordinates at the gravesite. What better person to create such havoc when he could shake off any suspicion by putting the law and focus on someone else?

A member of the ton? Someone who had sat in the opera box not far from her? No one would suspect a high-ranking man to be capable of such vile acts.

Whoever this was, he'd taken the time to light several candles within the marble structure, placed in the four corners. To call the powers of the directions? Possibly.

And then all her thoughts coalesced into one frigid assurance when the soft candlelight glinted off a gold ring on his hand. It was only this afternoon that she'd seen the same thing and had ignored it by thinking it was his hair in the sunlight, dismissing the man and speaking directly to her hostess. He'd been disheveled, and she had left him and his mother in the parlor to then head to the rookery. The sound of those pounding hooves a street over from her carriage could have been him rushing to pin that letter to the door Franny had to have opened to him on the fateful night when he took her life. When he took the very essence of who she was under the grime of what life had thrown at her.

"Mr. Havershall." Now would be the very worst time to show that if there was anyone she might be physically afraid of, it would be this man who was not only several years her junior but also a burly man who she knew boxed in his leisure time.

Her words made him pause and she took the time to reach into her reticule and push the one thing that might not save her but at least would allow whoever found her body to finally end things with this horrible man.

She wasn't going down without a fight though.

"I know it's you. I'm not an idiot. I've had misgivings about you since the first night at the séance." That wasn't exactly true, and she wasn't a very good liar, but she would do her best. Now she just had to get him to talk.

"At least let me see the face of the man who thinks he can best me. Show yourself."

He stalked to his right, coming around the corner of the sarcophagus between them on the pedestal. She was quick to also move. They circled a couple of times before he lunged at her, knocking off his own mask.

Exposing that it was indeed Havershall, his face angry, his brow creased, sweat beading on his forehead and slicking his hair to his crimson cheeks.

"It's sweaty work being a horrible man, isn't it?" she said, knowing that it would only make him angrier but needing him unstable if she was to get out of this alive.

He shoved the lid of the sarcophagus at her with such force that it plunged to the floor at her feet, making her jump back and slam into the columbarium holding four different urns. They crashed to the floor and a cloud of ash rose, concealing her just long enough to pick up a piece of the broken pottery to hide behind her back.

"You killed your own wife to gain her powers? Surely, she loved you enough that she would have shared whatever she was capable of with you."

At this point it was just her talking, and she needed more. She needed to know why. And she needed a distraction because the door opened into the mausoleum, which meant she was never going to have enough time to escape if he was still standing.

"You've got it wrong, Coriander." He sneered her name, but she let it go as they had started the dance around the coffin again. He darted to the left this time, but she had been watching and didn't miss the pivot.

"How so? There is a slew of people right outside this door who know where I am, Rook, so how will you get away with this? What's your next move? I made mine, now give me yours. Or are you not certain what comes next?"

His eyes bulged and his hands clenched. She began gathering his rage and his hatred to her and focusing it into the shard of the urn she'd taken from the ground. It hurt her head to do this, but a whole lot more would hurt besides her head if she couldn't pull it off. Right before her was the very thing that might be able to get her out of this mess and out of the mausoleum if only she could get enough energy to make it happen.

He yelled and threw himself forward just as she released a spell she hadn't done since her little cat passed away when she was ten. Reanimation of a corpse was never a good thing, especially if one did not practice often. Her poor cat had not known where it was or how to function and her mother had had to help her let it rest. Reanimating a two-hundred-year-old woman was definitely harder, but she tried.

The corpse of a long-dead matriarch raised her skeletal arm and caught Havershall in the crotch as he dove over her resting place. He grunted and rolled off to the side, giving Cory a precious moment to redirect the energy and have the woman sit up. But she couldn't get her to walk. The skeleton kept hitting the side of the coffin and then collapsing, and that's what gave him time to snatch Cory and yank her head back by her hair while shoving the shard of the urn up against her throat.

"Enough with your atrocities. I did not want to use the women's magic. I want all magic gone. I do not want it to be transferred to any new generations. By bleeding it off the women I am able to make sure it does not seep into a new person and change their very being. Your husband had come to the realization that the Egyptians would use the embalming to save organs in the vessels. But for someone who had magic, they had a special vessel to hold their essence and be able to transfer it to the next in line to boost that woman's powers and abilities. Some people are born with the blood, but they too can be enhanced. Elsbeth and her coven had shared that they would be resurrecting the old ways so they could eventually live among the world without fear of people knowing their true selves, the abominations that they are. So, I killed them and took their essence. Every one of them. I tried to get my wife to tell me everyone who needed to die, but she would not and so I took her life and waited to see who came to collect. And then I took her life too. She thought she could save herself by telling me any and everyone else who could go before her."

Cory tried to swallow around the blade shoved into the soft flesh of her throat. So, he was working down a list. Had Franny given up every woman who had magic in the area in order to save her own life?

Even if she had, Cory would never fault her. This man was at fault. This man was the abomination. This man was going down.

The corpse fell out of the coffin with Cory's last burst of energy to save herself, and she knew that the end was near. She'd see Ezra again. She'd be able to rest and perhaps in the Summerlands, she'd be able to grow all the plants and flowers that she wished she could say goodbye to now.

But not today.

She pushed back as hard as she could, throwing all her weight into the thrust, wanting to make Havershall hit the wall hard enough to drop the shard.

He laughed at her weakness and then grunted when the door flew open and whacked him not only in the back of the head. His whole body vibrated with the impact.

"Cory, my goddess." Flossie leaned panting against the wall. "You shook the whole freaking cemetery with whatever spell you did not two minutes ago. Someone fell in the hole with Timothy and crashed into his coffin. It was a disaster, but it let me know where you were."

Havershall lay on the ground at their feet as Esther showed up in the doorway with a frying pan of all things and a look on her face that could have stopped a giant at twenty paces.

"Where is he? I'm going to smash his head in."

"There's no need, Esther." Flossie pointed to the man on the floor. "He's done in by a door, the stupid buffoon. I bet Cory was just a breath away from taking him down to the depths, but I saved her the trouble by slamming him into the far wall."

"Good work," Esther said, resting the pan on her shoulder.

"What were you planning on doing with that, Esther, and how did you get it?" Cory asked.

Esther brought the pan forward and ran a soft caress over the edge of the skillet. "I may be a paragon of good manners now, Ms. Whitlock, but I didn't grow up that way. And Henry was happy to put it under the box up front when I asked him very nicely. I didn't have to use it, but I think I'll thank him again for stashing it away for me. Nicely." She winked at Cory, and Cory could do nothing but laugh with the real last of her breath before she collapsed to the floor.

Larkin was there, though, to catch her before she made impact. He grabbed her around the waist and cradled her head in his broad hand. As he stared down into her eyes her hand lifted to brush his strong jaw.

"Are you okay?" he asked in a low voice.

"Mmm-hmm." She was lost, so lost in his gaze that she almost missed everyone turning their back as he dipped down to touch his lips to hers. It was brief, it was barely a touch, and yet it tingled in every single piece of her body. Electricity, akin to the zap she'd endured from the various machines that roamed her house, ran through her every nerve ending. When he pulled back and brought her to her feet, flush with his body, Flossie ruined it by giggling.

Cory was quick to step away, but Larkin trailed his fingers down her arm, clasping her hand and not letting her get far.

"I'm thinking we should bring in the police now before the scoundrel wakes and before there are too many questions." He feathered his fingers over the back of her hand and it zipped along her spine. She was going to combust if she didn't get away from him.

But as soon as she tugged her hand away from his she felt the loss in the core of her soul.

They stepped out of the mausoleum and made their way down the path. Leaving Harry and Esther to watch over Havershall was a no-brainer. They would not let him get away.

Flossie chattered incessantly as they made their way back to the funeral site. She wasn't wrong, things were still a mess as people tried to yank Beulah Fetheringworth out of the grave. She kept screaming and cursing in a very unlady-like way.

Inspector Parker's gaze snapped up as soon as they rounded the corner at another mausoleum. His stare did not do the things that Larkin's did, but it did put her on guard.

"I think I should do this myself," she said, untangling herself from Larkin and Flossie at her sides.

"Be careful." Flossie flapped a hand at her and then wrapped her fingers around Larkin's elbow. Cory turned when she remembered he would be perfectly capable of handling himself.

"Inspector Parker, may I have a moment of your time?"

He looked over her head and dropped his shoulders in a sigh. "Why do I have a feeling I might not like what you have to say?"

"Well, if you go over two rows and up four mausoleums, I believe you will find what you've been looking for all along. Esther is there, and I'm sure she'd be happy to help you keep the real villain in this story under control while you remand him into custody for at least five murders in the area. I believe I have some evidence that you would want if I can bring it by tomorrow?"

One of the few times she'd ever walk into a station without feeling like the world was out to get her. And she had that recording in her reticule. Of course, it would need some serious editing if she could figure out how to do that, but it was a confession all on its own and perhaps if they put her in a room with the dastardly man who had tried to rid the world of one of its greatest gifts, he'd talk, knowing that not only did he not ruin her, he'd made her stronger.

Checkmate.

EPILOGUE

Tinkering with Ezra's pocket watch proved more difficult than Coriander expected. Despite years of experience altering his mechanical devices, the intricate mechanism and the trace of ancient, foreign magic engraved onto the delicate gears exceeded her skill level and left her feeling like a first-year witch. In the end, tinkering with the inspector's mind was the best and last option.

Coriander returned to the Metropolitan Police headquarters the following day, her drawings and Ezra's pocket watch in hand, to meet with the special inspector. For once, he seemed happy to see her. Though the sentiment was short-lived once she played the recording of Havershall's confession.

A sheen of sweat coated Parker's skin; his face took on a sickly pallor as the color drained from his cheeks at the first mention of magic. He collapsed in his chair when Coriander provided the proof of its existence he required. She hated tampering with anyone's mind—especially if they had undergone a compulsion spell before. One experience with that particular brand of magic was enough to muddy the mind and affect the results. She needed him to believe in the magic in order for him to believe in the legitimacy of the recording. Which was why she spent so much time and energy performing parlor tricks for Parker. She was exhausted and perspiring by the time the inspector was convinced. Once Havershall's words rang true, she used the last of her reserves to pull the magical elements from Parker's memory.

When presented with the circumstantial evidence Coriander collected and Havershall's damning admission, Special Inspector Parker was left with little choice but to agree that the scoundrel he'd arrested was indeed the correct person, and that sent shock waves through all levels of London society.

The Chronicle had been the first paper to run with a story that rivaled even the grisliest Penny Dreadful. "Jack's Back." The headline fed London's morbid fascination with the gruesome side of death and whipped the city into a frenzy. While the details of the article were speculation at best, the similarities between Havershall and London's infamous murderer were more than enough to convict the socialite in the court of public opinion. Even though only two of the five were prostitutes, the lure of making them parallel was too much for the ton to ignore.

The Morning Post picked up the story and ran away with it. New Name, Old Method. The reporter wove a delicate web with his words, connecting each detail together until he trapped Havershall in the article's sticky center. From the first letter of the killer's moniker—R for Ripper, R for Rook, to his choice of seedy locations and vulnerable victims, Havershall sealed his fate.

His insistence that magic not only existed but tainted the very souls of each and every Londoner was—according to *The Chronicle*—the ravings of a lunatic and all but assured his room and board at Bedlam.

Coriander knew the ruin of her friend's reputation and desecration of her memory was as necessary as it was painful. She took solace in that fact that Franny lived her life on her town terms and never much cared for the opinion of anyone outside of her coven.

"Coriander, it's time." The timber of Larkin's rich, velvet voice pulled her from her morbid thoughts and back into the present.

Larkin refused to leave her side, taking up residence in one of the few spare bedrooms at Elmcroft Manor just down the hall from her own, until he was certain she was safe and Havershall was under lock and key. His presence was a welcome distraction from the circus that surrounded the trial. She'd grown comfortable with his presence, looked forward to the wit and bite of their banter, the way he challenged her and found a way to touch her while maintaining propriety at every opportunity.

As much as it pained her to admit it, she would miss him. He could never replace her dear departed husband, but with each passing day Larkin convinced her a little more that he just might fill the hole in her heart that Ezra left behind.

And now he was leaving her too.

"So soon?" Coriander asked, despite having marked each day of the month they spent together in the pages of her journal.

"We discussed this." Larkin navigated the small space between the couch and wooden table as he crossed the parlor and joined her at the fireplace. "The Society of Paraphysical Research is meeting in Glasgow in four days' time. If I don't leave now, I won't reach the city in time. Even pushing the horse, riding at top speed, there is a chance I won't make it. I'll have to stop to feed and water the horse, allow him to rest."

"And you as well, Larkin." Coriander shifted one corner of her mouth, offering him a half smile that did little to hide the concern she was certain reflected in her eyes.

She knew that the tall, broad, broody, domineering man that loomed over her was more than capable of taking care of himself, and yet she knew that she would worry about him anyway. He planned to attend the meeting in Glasgow without an invitation from his employers in the hopes of confirming the Order of the Hammer's resurrection started and ended with Havershall and any risk to Coriander, or any other woman with magical inclinations, had been eliminated with Havershall's incarceration.

If the Order of the Hammer had in fact returned, they posed a real and serious threat. Until they received those assurances the order hadn't taken root somewhere else, none of them were safe.

Not even Larkin.

"Are you worried something will happen to me, Coriander?" Larkin teased. Something that seemed to be a favorite pastime of his in light of the revelation of her budding feelings toward him. He returned her smile, though his was genuine, and spared a cursory glance around the room. Seemingly satisfied they were alone, he took her hand in his. "There is very little in this world that could take me away from you, Coriander, but your safety is one of them."

He raised her hand to his lips, a promise to return falling from them before he brushed them across his knuckles with a look in his eyes that promised something more upon his return.

Her breath hitched, chest expanding as much as possible within the confines of the damnable corset as she struggled to pull more air into her lungs. "You have to go," she rasped, her voice unrecognizable even to her own ears from the effect Larkin had on her.

"I do." His fingertips brushed hers, prolonging the release of her hand from his grasp. With a parting glance over his shoulder, he made his retreat from the parlor and Elmcroft Manor.

Coriander watched from the front window as he mounted his horse, seated himself in the saddle, and rode down the drive, wondering what it would be like to hear Larkin speak those two words under different circumstances.

As if called by the sound of church bells, imaginary or not, Flossie strolled into the parlor with Esther on her heels carrying a tray of tea, cakes, and three of her favorite teacups.

Esther was among Coriander's most trusted confidants, moving from servant to friend not long after she first arrived at Elmcroft. Ezra had been certain the two would get along famously, just as Coriander had been certain Flossie would see her worth and welcome her into their circle the same way she had.

And she had. If not before Esther's willingness to wield a cast iron pan as a weapon, then certainly after it.

"Is that lemon cake, Esther, and my bergamot blend?" Coriander asked, pushing her gardening journal and grimoire aside to make room for the service tray on the table.

"There aren't many troubles that can't be eased with a cup of strong tea and slice of sweet cake." Esther set about pouring the tea and serving up cake for the three of them before settling into the armchair opposite Coriander.

"I suppose you'll be on your way back to your estate soon. I imagine your dear husband has been missing you something terrible." Esther sipped her tea before setting it back on the table and reaching for her cake.

Larkin hadn't exactly made his intentions known, but they seemed clear enough to Coriander. With a desirable suitor secured, she was certain Flossie would return home as well.

"Yes, I suppose he is." Flossie's lips pursed as if her words, along with her tea, soured on her tongue. The delicate porcelain cup clinked against its saucer as she set them on the table with enough force to crack the china. "Though with Larkin in Glasgow for an undetermined amount of time, it may be best if I extend my stay at Elmcroft."

"Oh, that would be lovely, cousin. Wouldn't it, Esther?" She glanced at her friend seated opposite her, whose eyes had taken on the shape of the saucers holding their teacups, and drowned her amusement in a long sip of her bergamot blend.

Esther enjoyed Flossie's company as much as she did. The gaggle of servants that accompanied her, not so much. Though when Esther's eyes softened at the mention of Flossie's coachman, Coriander suspected that he might be the exception.

"It's decided then. I'll have Henry send word my stay here at Elmcroft will be extended." Flossie's stiff nod and sharp tone raised other suspicions for Coriander—that there might be more to her cousin's visit than she let on.

But that was a problem for another day. Coriander had no desire to borrow trouble. She'd had more than enough to last her a lifetime.

A break in the clouds that draped over the London sky like a heavy curtain cast beams of light through the parlor windows and drew Coriander's attention to her beloved garden and the plants she'd neglected in her pursuit of the Rook.

"It looks as though the weather may turn. I think I'll take my tea in the garden." She warmed her cup, added a cube of sugar, and after a quick stir, excused herself from the parlor and the company of her friends.

Her boots crunched along the pea gravel as she sipped her tea and soaked up the sun's rejuvenating rays as she meandered among the many varieties of beautiful but deadly plants. White oleander popped against the deep purple hues of deadly nightshade. Ruby foxgloves towered over the burnt-orange azaleas.

Coriander balanced her teacup in one hand, reached into the slot hidden in the seam of her skirt with the other, and retrieved the funeral biscuit as she strolled along the paths between the monkshood, castor bean, angel's trumpet, and water hemlock; each plant hiding its gruesome nature behind glorious blooms. She traced her thumb over the monogrammed icing. Curiosity, and perhaps her own grim nature, had gotten the better of her and driven her to test the toxicity of the biscuit.

She took a large bite of the biscuit, savoring the buttery cookie as she chewed. She washed the mouthful down, the black tea bitter against the sweetness of the icing.

A rueful smile settled on her lips. Had their roles been reversed it was an opportunity she would not have missed. Given her proficiency in potions, using the biscuit as a possible back-up plan for murder could have been brilliant.

"If he'd thought out his moves better, he could have taken me off the board altogether. Amateur." With a smile on her face, she danced her fingers along the deadly blooms as she finished her tea. She gave the remaining morsel of what could have been a lethal biscuit if he'd had any brains one last examination before popping it in her mouth. "Check and possible mate."

Hopefully life was about to take a turn for the better.

Rachel and I hope you loved our first book together and will come back for more!

If you need something to fill your time before the next Coriander adventure is done, please look for us on the web at:

Rachel Rawlings www.rachelrawlings.com
Misty Simon www.mistysimon.com

Made in the USA
Middletown, DE
14 October 2024